SpellCast from Darkness

Beyond the Shadows, Volume 2

Shanna Robillard

Published by Shanna Robillard, 2022.

SPELLCAST FROM DARKNESS

First edition. February 2, 2022.

ISBN: 978-0578367699

Written by Shanna Robillard.

Table of Contents

This book is dedicated to the fans who demanded more about Michael and Celie. Thank you for helping me bring this story to life...

Also from the Author

Beyond the Shadows Trilogy
Beyond the Shadows
SpellCast from Darkness
Against the Coming Dark

The Brimstone Court Novels
Book One: The Darkest Echo
Book Two: Consumed in the Dark
Book Three: Burned in the Dark (Coming June 2025)
Book Four: Wanted in the Dark (Coming Summer/Fall 2025)
Book Five: Falling in the Dark (Coming Winter 2025)
Book Six: Wounded in the Dark (Coming Spring 2026)
Book Seven: Salvation in the Dark (Coming Summer 2026)

Standalone Books
A Tale by Moonlight
The Seven Lives of May Levesque
Queen of the High Seas
Folklore: The Beginning
Rising Phoenix

Warning

This book contains content that may be triggering to some readers.

Amnesia
Burning
Car Accident
Cheating (in a Relationship)
Choking
Death
Drowning
Ghosts
Home Invasion
Snakes
Stalking
Suffocating
Threats
Violence

Note

This book contains multiple foreign languages.
Many words and phrases are defined
alongside their pronunciation at the end of the book.

Prologue

The Note

To the vampire—

You are an abomination. An unholy cursed thing. You bring evil to this world, and we mean to see your ruin.

Lest you forget who we are, we were born into this world centuries ago at the behest of those who would see your kind destroyed. Our drive, our ambition is to see the end of you and all like you. There is no negotiating this. No one can change this. We would see it culminate with your death and the death of all you ungodly creatures. Then we can finally take our leave.

Speak unto us and perish. Take us into thine eyes, and we will smite thee. We will be the cause of your endless pain and infinite suffering. Your existence will be your undoing. Your days are finite. Take what little refuge you have in the time you have left.

We are coming.

The Spellcasters

"Hey hon? Have you seen this letter?"

"What letter?"

"This one." I flung the letter around in the air, the fluttering making a flapping sound meant to grab his attention.

Michael Hawkins came out from the kitchen, drying his hands off on a dish towel. My vampire was still more human than most and had just finished washing our dishes from dinner—a *real* dinner. We still had those from time to time, especially on date night. I offered him a glass of Pinot Noir, which he gladly accepted along with the letter I handed to him.

"What is this?"

"I'm not sure. It came with the mail today." When I was out in town earlier, I had picked up our mail from a post office box. We never had anything delivered to the house. Besides, it wasn't like anyone could find it anyway.

Michael took a moment to read through the letter. "'The SpellCasters'...? I've never heard of them...?" I watched as he smelled the letter, checking the paper quality, and examining the envelope. "This is vellum, perhaps from the 19th century? How intriguing..."

"Should we call Watson, Mr. Holmes? Is this brand-new information?"

"Very new—surprising, too, as these people indicate they've been around for centuries..."

"Hmm... Any chance this is just a prank? You should talk with Xander: maybe he's punking you."

"Not really his style." Michael lit up and pointed his finger upwards, an idea sparking in his brain. "Ah! I do have someone I can ask about it, though."

"Oh really?" I pouted and raised an eyebrow. "Am I not the only vamp in your life?"

He grimaced. "Now stop that. I told you I hate that term."

"What? Vamp?"

Michael groaned in response.

"Vamp, vamp, vamp!" I laughed with glee before squealing as Michael stalked over and chased me around the table. In a second, he had swept me up and was kissing me passionately, leaving me breathless.

"I love you, but you really know all of my damn buttons, don't you?"

I just giggled in response. He growled and threw me over his shoulder, carting me up the stairs to the bedroom. I yelped playfully as he smacked my ass and gave it a squeeze for good measure.

Say what you want, but no one said foreplay had to be serious.

After that, the letter didn't come up for quite some time...

Chapter One

The Arrival

The SpellCasters arrived on a Thursday.

It was morning, and the sun shone warmly across the front steps of Michael's house just outside Bantum. Michael and I were preparing for a long weekend with his best friend, Xander and my best friend, Kat. They were going to join us on a camping trip into the Ozarks, and we had been gearing up, packing bags, and the like. To be honest, life had been singularly average for us both—or as average as two vampires could have it.

Wait—you're probably confused about what happened before. Sorry! Let me explain.

After I found my way back to him, Michael explained he had tried to protect me the best way that he knew how: using his abilities to convince me that I had simply been dreaming. He tried to convince me that I had been dreaming about everything from Devlin Raines to being a vampire. He knew I could get regular transfusions to account for the blood lust, knowing the hospital would be unable to determine the cause of it. Ultimately, he wanted me to have as normal a life as possible. His plan was that he would just keep an eye on me, and if I grew out of control, he would come to me. Then he mind-wiped Kat and left us both at home.

Did he have misgivings about doing it? Of course. Did he hope that everything would work out and that I would find a way through his abilities? Absolutely. Was he apologetic once I threatened to slam his head through a wall? Naturally. But once the two of us were reunited, we reconnected on every level—*every level.*

It had been months since I came home, and—to be honest—it wasn't just Michael's house anymore. It was *our* house. I had moved in, bringing myself and many of my creature comforts to be with him in his unique and shielded home: blankets and pillows, tarot cards and runes, vinyl albums, and a plethora of photography. I was living with him and loving every minute of it. Every day and night I spent with him, I learned more about him—and about myself.

Discovering your vampire self is an amazing thing, one that I could have only dreamed about before. I had more time to learn and develop my skills, using my abilities to help Michael with anything and everything I could. Did you know that I could manifest ghosts? Yes! My new abilities intertwined with my existing capabilities, and my psychic nature became ethereal manifestations. I had spoken with my ancestors, including my grandmother, and it was incredibly rewarding. None of the ghosts were malevolent or held any negative energies; they were just lost souls in need of guidance or comfort.

Michael also continued to involve me in his life. He showed me more of the antique business, bringing me in as a partner. Xander had found the government less...fulfilling after the dealings with the cult, so he quit and became a full partner in the business as well. We continued to train together in case any Sons or Daughters of the Savior decided to come back for another go at him or us. When we weren't working or training, we were enjoying experiencing hiking in nature, going out for dinner, or just staying in to watch a movie. Spending my life with Michael was rewarding in so many ways.

Yet the biggest and best part of our connection was that he introduced me to Ginny. I cannot even begin to describe how honored I was to finally meet her and how special it made me feel. She was stunning, a breathtaking older beauty with flowing snow-white hair and deep golden eyes the color of honey. She was also beautiful within, so kind and generous. She gave me her stamp of approval, and I've never felt more respected in my entire life.

Oh, and if you're still wondering if everything I told you happened, I assure you it did. That was *no* dream.

Okay—back to my story!

I had just gotten my bags downstairs when there was a noise at the front door, a knocking sound. As per usual, no one should be able to find the house but the two of us or those we invite specifically. That was part of Michael's abilities: shielding the house from outside visitors. Curious, I went to investigate.

Four strangely alluring and utterly striking individuals were standing there on our doorstep.

I was greeted first by a tall Eastern man—Indian? Pakistani? His thin, wiry frame was garbed in loose gray linens. His salt-and-pepper chin-length hair was wind-swept, yet his face was youthful and strong, his nose large and his lips thin. His eyes were the color of a darkened sky after lightning strikes.

"Cecelia Moore?" He bent his head in my direction, a smile on his curious face. "Are you she?"

When this man spoke, his tone was disarming: calm, smooth, a hint of British aristocracy lingering in the air. I immediately wanted to smile in response to his polite query. Mentally noting my misgivings about anyone finding the house, I shook my head, keeping my reaction in check.

With this smooth-talking man were three women, all of varying appearance but none less a fantastic beauty than the other. The first one was tall, lithe, and sinewy, her frame dressed in worn brown leather and rugged biker boots. Red was her color, from her fiery, stick-straight bobbed hair to her painted fingernails and pouty cherry lips. Her face was angular, stunning, with heavy black eyeshadow that made her blue eyes pierce my soul. She narrowed her eyes at me, and I felt immediate misgivings.

Next to her stood a mermaid on land. Silken, wavy, pale blonde tresses hung down to graze the back of her thighs. She was pale, her heart-shaped face painted in shimmering pastel blues and purples, her wide, round eyes a frosty green like frozen seafoam. Her siren dress was silken and silver, bearing iridescent glints of lavender, and barely skimming her frame as it hugged every curve. Her snow-white feet were bare and dirty. I was reminded of a faerie of the coastal waters, but I knew it belied a cold and biting spirit.

The final woman was an earthy goddess: rich, velvet mahogany skin, bright golden eyes, long black hair that hung in tightly-coiled spiral curls down to her mid-back. She was voluptuous and womanly: her green and gold-colored silk robes were cinched tightly at her tiny waist, accentuating her hourglass shape. Her round face was smooth and unblemished, and delicate gold piercings in her septum, nostrils, and eyebrows. Despite her warm appearance, though, I felt terrorized by her gaze, her aureate eyes seeming to burn deep into my core. This goddess was truly a demoness in disguise.

I blinked and looked at him again. "Um, who's asking?"

"My name is Pavan. Are you the woman we seek?"

"That depends, *Pavan*. What the hell are you and your supermodels doing on our front step?" Annoyed at the interruption, I used that feeling to hide my fright. I silently called for Michael, and in a flash, he was standing next to me, his fists clenched, ready to fight. He slowly stepped around me to make himself visible in the doorway.

"We are The SpellCasters. These are my associates: Brigit, Rusalka, and Meyana." He gestured from the red head to the earth goddess. "If I recall correctly, we *did* tell you we were coming."

Crap—that damn weird letter.

"Yeah, we got a memo. Thanks for the heads up."

"I'm surprised you are still here?" He had the audacity to look concerned. I raised an eyebrow. "You know we have come to dispatch you."

I smirked at them and glanced at Michael. He addressed Pavan directly. "How do you plan on doing that, exactly? What kind of army do you bring? Because that's what it will take, sir."

Pavan chuckled, as did the women; although, the redhead chose to cross her arms and glare at us instead. "No, no. We're here to enact our spells of vanquishing. As our letter stated, now that you have seen us, witnessed us, we shall eradicate you from this earth." He gave a small bow. "This is our truth."

The entire conversation was getting too surreal for me. "You do realize that we're vampires, right? You know—teeth, blood, throat-ripping vampires?" I scrunched up one side of my face. "It would take a lot more than a 'sashay' and a 'little turn on the catwalk.'"

"Precisely."

At that moment, he swept his left hand slightly—his first two fingers pointing outward—and each of the 'SpellCasters' pushed through the last of the barriers, walking right into the house. Michael and I, respectively, began to back up, prepared to defend ourselves. Each of SpellCaster was chanting, separate sets of words and hand motions to coincide with each of their magic specialties; yet none of them attempted to attack us—not physically, anyway. Their chanting grew louder, and they stood before us in power poses like magical, wrathful villains—hands twitching, arms and wrists bending. I stood transfixed, ready to unleash my most inner demonic-like self to protect us.

Suddenly, it was too late: before either of us could register what was happening, they had cast their spells on us.

It began with the earthy goddess, Meyana, who spelled us both in place. She dropped to one knee and whispered low and strong, her hands gesturing across the ground. She twisted them slowly up and over each other, rising higher until she was standing again. Large vines and dark roots grew from the ground, wrapping around our legs and arms. I felt them wrap around my wrists in a flash, far faster than either of us could tear them free. Small leaves and shoots burst out from the vines, and the scent of green herbs and heady, sweet flowers filled the room. I couldn't move, my arms pinned at my sides. I looked to my right to find Michael struggling next to me.

What are they doing to us?

I don't know, but I don't like this. He glanced at me. *Can you break free? Can you transform?*

I tried, but the bindings were too tight. I felt my teeth elongate, but I couldn't tilt my head forward far enough to bite through the bindings. I tried to transform into my panther shape, but with every shift of my limbs, the vines dug deep into my flesh.

Damnit! No, they're— Argh! They're cutting into me when I try to shift! I sighed in frustration. *I'm not bendy enough to get close enough to bite through them. You?*

He wrestled against the bindings, gnashing and writhing, but there was no success. *No.*

As the vines wove tighter around us, the siren, Rusalka murmured seductively. Her hair shimmered as she approached us, her bare feet quietly crossing the floor. There was something about her movements that made me both hate her and love her. Curling her hands over and around each other, she then brought them together, cupped them and slowly extended them outward, releasing a current of gentle water from her hands at Michael. He continued to wrestle as it reached him, the water evaporating into a mist as it came into contact, covering his form like a netting that enveloped him.

At that moment, I felt something inside me loosen, then break, snapping sharply within my mind. The only thing I knew was that it was shared between us, as if a tether we had to each other no longer connected us. His voice was gone from inside my head, and I felt empty—alone: I was vulnerable in a fresh, new way. All this time, I had grown accustomed to him being with me, and his absence was heartbreaking.

I struggled furiously, desperate to confirm what she had done to him. I glanced sharply, repeatedly, from him to her, looking for a sign of changes. The waif-like faerie-bitch smiled deviously at me, her arms coming to rest at her sides.

Michael's bindings came undone, and he dropped to the floor, staring up at the SpellCasters in bewilderment. The earth goddess, Meyana, stooped down and reached out, taking Michael gently by the chin. I watched, incredulous, as she lifted his gaze to hers, and after a moment, his own face softened into a smile. She smiled back at him and then glanced at me, angling her head slightly to the side. Her own smile transformed into one so sinister, I swore it would be etched into my memory forever.

"No!" I shouted and resumed struggling with all my might. Nothing worked. I shouted and screamed, called to him, and cursed them. I willed myself to change, trying to force myself to shapeshift, but my body refused. I pleaded for Michael with my mind, but he wasn't there. He was right in front of me, and I couldn't hear him or sense him anymore. I yelled his name, but he refused to look at me.

He only had eyes for Meyana.

"What have you done? WHAT HAVE YOU DONE?" I cried, tears pouring down my face as I wailed and screamed. My rage burned me from the outside inward, and my sorrow drowned me from the inside out. In front of him, Meyana tilted her head back and laughed.

While I was distracted with my soul tearing in two, Pavan had closed his eyes, mumbling something fast in short, low bursts punctuated with loud incantations. When he stopped, it caught my attention, and I knew something horrible was coming. Without warning, he outstretched his hands and forced a steady gust of wind in my direction. Closing my eyes instinctively, I felt the blast hit me, cold and intimidating, seeping into my skin and burning through to my bones like a nitrogen-fueled fire. My mind began to fog, my thoughts and vision clouding over.

What was this sorcery? Why? What had they done to Michael? Why were they trying to destroy us? What are they doing to me? To us? What are...what are they...what...what is going on?

My eyes flashed open. Four people surrounded me, all exotic and astonishingly attractive, with an unbelievably handsome man on the floor to my right.

Who is the man on the floor? Who are these people?

I shook my head, and my vision cleared, the blur dissipating. I wasn't capable of processing what I was witnessing or experiencing. *Where am I? What is happening? Who...* I shook my head and blinked. *Who am I?*

Vines and roots were wrapped around me, and I couldn't move. I struggled, but the bindings wouldn't budge. Intense fear gripped me; I was unsure of my fate or what would become of me. *What is going on? Are they trying to kill me? Is this where I'm going to die?*

I watched as a tall woman with fiery red hair laughed and laughed, cackling maniacally as she twisted her hands over and over again in rapid succession, a glowing intensity building within them from her movements. Even without understanding, I could still recognize when I should be frightened—and I was petrified. The red woman brought her hands up to her face, gently blowing into them. Suddenly, she shoved her hands outward, sending a firestorm bursting forth from within them. I saw the fiery blast coming at me and shut my eyes.

Never had I felt anything so powerful. My stomach seemed to drop inside my belly like I was thrust onto an unseen rollercoaster, sinking fast and quick. I could feel my hair flying in all directions, winds whipping around my face. Heat burned my face, flames fanning my cheeks, and the warmth thrashed around me, charring my skin in a tornado of fire. My clothes were pulling and tugging at me all over, snug and loose, tight and baggy. I felt myself falling—end over end—and nothing could stop it. Fear enveloped me, and I began to scream.

As quickly as it had started, I felt myself hit the ground with a thud, pain radiating through to my bones, and everything stopped. Lying on my side, I winced, slowly opening my eyes: my whole right side hurt. Blinking in quick succession, I was afraid I would be stuck with my fuzzy vision. I pushed up, leaning heavily on my right arm and shook my head, wincing again at the pain.

My vision finally cleared, leaving me dumbstruck. I was on a grassy field, a rock wall to my left leading toward the horizon. Sitting upright, I surveyed my surroundings. A lake was behind me, just beyond some trees, small waves lapping at the shoreline like nature's music. I could hear it and the sound comforted me for reasons I couldn't fathom. The sky was a brilliant blue with delicate silver clouds dappled throughout its magnificence. Small rays of sunshine came out and blinded me with their golden casts. A chill breeze blew across the grass, and I shivered. This was a peaceful, gorgeous place.

But where was I? What was this place? How did I get here?

Better yet, who was I?

I couldn't remember my name or how I got to this place. With no idea of where I was or who I was, at best I was terrified; at worst, I was a zombie. I stood up to take in my situation and look for clues, stumbling as I found my footing. My clothes were worn, but they were definitely mine based on the fit. My shirt had a logo of a mountain on it, but no descriptive text. My black boots were mine, and I could wiggle my toes in them, so I knew my feet worked. I checked my jean pockets and found nothing in them except a now broken cell phone.

How was I going to make it 24 hours without anything on me? No money? No identification? *Might as well go to the police and turn myself in, see if they can help me...*

So that's exactly what I did.

Now, you might be wondering how I even remembered what a cell phone was or police, but I can assure you that part of my memory was intact. It was just me that I couldn't remember; it was everything and anything about myself that I couldn't place. I could tell you how to tie my shoe, but I definitely couldn't tell you my birthdate or what color my eyes were—not without a mirror, anyway.

"Let's get walking," I muttered to myself.

I picked a direction and started out, finding a worn dirt path with what looked like tire tracks. Following the path and the sun, I headed west, hoping that I could find some sort of farmhouse or sign of civilization. Eventually I came to a paved road, and it took me north. Cars streamed past me and some occasionally honked. I had one person stop and offer me help, but I simply confirmed I was headed in the right direction for the closest police station.

By nightfall I had incredibly painful feet and calves, but I had reached a small town. Local authorities picked me up and took me to the station, giving my feet a welcome respite. I was happy to reach something resembling safety. This was where I sat, wrapped in a blanket and sipping a cup of hot cocoa, contemplating what life I had before this, and trying to answer their questions—including why I didn't sound like them.

You see, these weren't the police; they were the Garda.

And I was in Roscommon, Ireland.

Chapter Two

Betrayal

Michael woke from a nightmare to the feather-light touch of velvet against his naked skin.

The sultry sensation traced itself from his left shoulder, then down across his chest. It circled his nipple and lightly stroked across it, causing him to sharply intake a breath. He didn't open his eyes for fear it was another dream, but then the touch moved slowly down his abdomen. It stopped inches below his navel, making lazy circles, then suddenly dove down further still and wrapped around him completely. He gasped at the intimacy and opened his eyes.

Golden, shimmering eyes gazed delightfully into his own. A luscious pair of blood-red lips smiled for him. The scent of jasmine filled the air. Rich brown skin the color of burnt sienna, a pair of bare breasts dangled temptingly over his chest, a striking contrast to his own creamy skin.

Meyana...

She pressed her voluptuous naked body against his, bringing her right leg up and over his thighs. She began to writhe seductively in unspoken yearning, asking him—no, begging him to touch her. As she slid her hand along his cock, he eagerly complied, ripping away the sheet that separated them and groaning at the feel of her flesh against his. Michael grabbed her exquisite backside and squeezed. She smiled for him and tilted her head back.

Then Meyanna pushed herself up and drew her leg over him, straddling him. With one hand on his hip bone, she used her other hand to grasp him and slide him across the softest parts of her. She moaned loudly and grabbed his hands, placing them on her breasts. Michael teased her nipples and then sat up to take one into his mouth. His tongue danced across her bare skin, and she moaned again in pleasure.

Within moments, she had guided his cock so she could settle onto him, enclosing him in a tight, warm sheath. As she came down, she stretched her legs wider, taking him deep. Michael closed his eyes again and tilted his own head back as she began to ride him, leaning her body back to brace herself on his thighs. Her hips moved rhythmically like a wave, sliding herself over and over against his cock.

As he felt his building orgasm, she leaned forward, never stopping in her movements. His hands had been massaging her breasts and teasing her nipples, but now they grabbed hold of her hips and began urging her to go faster. One of her hands grabbed his chin, pulling his head back down, and he found himself staring into her eyes. She held him there, forcing him to watch her face as she began to rise higher, teetering closer to that blissful, chaotic edge. Indeed, she rode faster and soon became frantic, thrusting against him and pushing him to the brink. Suddenly she threw her head back and wailed, a scream of wild abandon, and he felt himself come as she pulsed around him, encircling him tighter.

Meyana...

She released his face and began to stroke his hair, kissing his brow, letting him release until he was spent. He fell backwards, his head hitting the pillow, and almost instantly fell back to sleep. The nightmares were gone.

"How long have we been together?" murmured Michael in her ear.

Meyana turned over in bed to face him. "Ages, $d\diamond$ (love). Ages. Why do you ask?"

"It feels new—yet...forever?"

"It can be both, $d\diamond$." She pressed her lips to his, their plump temptation stirring life within him yet again.

"You call me that. What does it mean?" He bent his head down to press a kiss on her collarbone. He used his tongue to lick a trail up her neck to her jawline. She shivered.

"$D\diamond$? In my language it means 'love.'"

"Is that what I am? Your love?"

"You are." She softly kissed his temple. "You are."

He smiled. Michael couldn't remember being so happy. He couldn't remember ever having been so comfortable and relaxed with someone. He couldn't remember...

Something? Someone?

There were those nagging thoughts again. They had been creeping into his subconscious these past couple of days, and he couldn't determine why or where they were coming from. They were simply there, randomly permeating his thoughts at times when he felt safest and most peaceful—like right now.

Like with Meyana.

He rolled her over, facing her away from him, and pulled her close. Her skin smelled like sweet flowers, and he nipped her shoulder. She pressed her ass up against him, rubbing and teasing, and making him harder than he already had been. Michael reached around her to slip a

21

finger into her silken, soft folds. She moaned low and sweet: it was his undoing. He grabbed her hip and slid his hand around and down her leg, lifting it. She parted for him, and he took advantage of the moment to gently push himself inside of her. She purred for him and reached back to grab his sleek hip. He groaned at the feel of her as his cock delved into her soft, tight core, and he reached around her to take one of her breasts into his hand. Rolling her nipples with his finger tips, he pinched slightly and smiled as she pushed back against him. As he continued to thrust against her, he heard her moan his name, and he drove faster, panting as he took them back into sweet ecstasy.

Meyana...

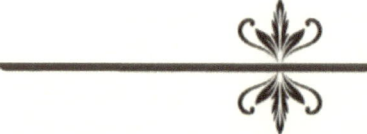

Days had passed since Michael had eaten—*really eaten.*

He needed a drink.

Slipping from the bed, Michael got dressed in a pair of dark blue jeans and a black t-shirt. As he crept to the door of his bedroom, he heard her stir.

"Where are you going, *d*◈?"

Holding the door open, Michael turned back to see her leaning up on one arm, his goddess among the tousled white sheets. He loved seeing her there, naked, full breasts and smooth, richly colored skin. Her long black hair was tousled in waves that fell over her right shoulder, and he wanted nothing more than to feel that hair against his bare skin.

"I have to feed, Mey."

"Not today. Come back to bed." She patted the sheets beside her and gave him a smoldering expression full of carnal promises. "I can give you something else to taste."

Michael felt the stirrings she always brought about in him, but he smiled and shook his head. "As much as I want to, I need to eat. I won't be much use to you if I don't."

Her own seductive smile turned into a pout. "You are sure then?"

"Unfortunately, yes."

"Okay, *d*◈. Hurry back to me." She rolled over and went back to sleep.

Michael went through the doorway and closed the door behind him. He made his way through the hallway and down the stairs to the main hall. Once there, he went around to the kitchen, checking to see if he had anything in his refrigerator to avoid leaving the house. Nothing. He went back to the main hall and glanced at the sitting room.

It was at that very moment a vision struck him.

A beautiful woman with alabaster skin and a button nose, warm auburn hair and brilliant green eyes, was sitting on his sofa with her feet tucked underneath her. She glanced at him and his breath caught in his throat. As she smiled lovingly, he felt her cast a warmth and light into the room that made his vampire heart ache. He instinctively stepped toward her, his hand reaching out to touch her—

Then it was gone. The vision faded away, and all of sudden he was gasping for air. He grimaced as if in pain, confused and disoriented.

What the hell was that? Who was that woman? Why did she smile at me that way? Why did seeing her affect me so?

Michael shook it off, taking several deep breaths to calm himself. Again, he had that nagging feeling that something was missing, and it was a feeling he couldn't shake. He looked around the hall, but nothing seemed amiss. The house felt cool and still smelled of the smoke from the fireplace the night before. Everything—from his tapestries to the suit of armor next to the base of the stairs—was all where it should be. Why couldn't he relax?

He felt a shiver roll across his body: it was his need to drink.

Leaving the house out the front door, Michael climbed into a large and boxy black SUV at the bottom of the front steps. Putting the key in the ignition, he hit the gas and kicked up gravel as he sped around the circular driveway. Reaching the large gates at the edge of the driveway, he stopped and put down his driver's side window. A breeze in the cool afternoon air swept across his arm as he reached out and pressed a large button to open the gates. Then he took off, pressing a button to put his window back up as he drove.

Once outside the property boundaries, he headed east until he reached Bantum City Hospital, turning into their parking lot and heading around the back. He found a parking spot close to the BCH Blood Bank office and parked. As Michael hopped out, something shiny fell from the car and clattered to the asphalt. He leaned down and picked it up, examining it closely.

It was a platinum ring band, small diamonds spaced out every five millimeters or so, and it bore three pyrope garnet inserts across the top.

Funny, I don't remember—

But he didn't finish his thought: he *did* remember this ring.

It belonged to Ginny, his oldest and dearest friend. She had promised it to him years ago. What was it she had said? "When you find them, you'll know...?"

Yes, that was it.

She had promised him this ring in exchange for a promise of his own: a promise that he would give it to the one person he could trust with his secret—a person he could trust with his life.

A person I can love eternally.

Why was this ring in his car? He didn't remember bringing it with him. In fact, he had no recollection of doing anything with the ring since Ginny had given it to him all those years ago.

He turned back to the SUV in confusion, then walked around to open the trunk, rummaging around through the items he found. It was primarily camping gear: head lamps, two sleeping bags, cooking pots, etc.. He was starting to get angry; he had no memory of this, no memory of camping or even *preparing* for camping. This was a disconcerting mystery—one that he wanted to solve—but when he tried to remember anything, the *only* thing he remembered was her—

Meyana...

Michael stepped back from the SUV, staring at the gear in his trunk. "What the hell is going on?"

Knowing that he couldn't go on much longer without feeding, Michael slammed the trunk shut, then made for the blood bank. He strode into the building and stopped at the front desk. As if using muscle memory, he swiftly produced his medical identification badge.

"Didn't bring the little lady with you this time?"

Startled, Michael shook his head. "Uh...no. No, she couldn't make it." Like the camping gear, he had no memory of bringing anyone to the Blood Bank before.

The nurse left the desk and went into the back. When she returned a few minutes later, she had a plain styrofoam cooler filled with pouches of O-positive blood. Michael accepted the bag and nodded to her in thanks. Turning, he took his leave and walked out, heading back to his SUV.

Climbing inside, Michael sat behind the steering wheel and closed the door. He reached over and opened the freezer bag, grabbing a pouch and tearing the corner of it with his teeth. Finally drinking, he relished the sweet, juicy liquid as it crossed his tongue and traveled down his throat. Pulling it back from his lips, he sighed, immediately gratified as his appetite was satiated. Then he sat for a moment, contemplating the few memories he had missing. He searched through his mind, but there was nothing.

After a few minutes, Michael shrugged it off and drove home.

"Have you come with me before?" He lay in bed, stroking Meyana's left arm draped over his chest.

Meyana was on his right and lifted her head from where it rested against his stomach, examining his face. They were both well spent after another round of lovemaking. She furrowed her brow, trying to understand the question.

"To the blood bank? No, *d*◈. I do not believe so."

"Interesting."

"Yes?"

"Well, the nurse there mentioned a 'little lady.' I had thought— Well, I thought she must have been referring to you."

Meyana smiled apologetically, and the air was perfumed with the fragrance of jasmine. "Oh... Yes, *now* I remember. I *do* recall a time, in fact, where I accompanied you. My apologies, *d*◈."

Michael smiled and nodded, seemingly reassured by her response. He relaxed and closed his eyes, comforted by her presence and well-satisfied from their recent activities. He began to nod off to sleep.

Suddenly he felt something against his left arm. He brushed it away, but it felt strange, like rope curling around him. He opened his eyes and saw vines beginning to wrap themselves around his forearm and legs. They peeked out from under the bed sheets, appearing to come from nowhere and heading to every extremity. Frantic, he tried to get them off his limbs, pushing, ripping, and tearing with no success. Each one he removed was fast replaced with another, as if there was a never-ending supply coming from within his bedding.

Fearing for her, Michael looked to his right and realized Meyana wasn't next to him. He looked to his left and froze; she was standing next to the bed in all her naked glory. Her voice was calm as she whispered words he didn't understand, moving her hands in ways he didn't recognize. She was gesturing outward from herself towards him, swaying her hips, her lips pursed in concentration, her eyes burning with golden fire.

As the vines continued to wrap around him, he called out to her.

"Meyana! Please! What are you doing? Why are you doing this?" His heart was in shambles: why would she want to do this to him?

Rather than answer, she looked into his eyes and smiled, and he stopped breathing. This was not the woman he had just made love to; this was not his earthy goddess. Her face was menacing, her blood-red lips pulled tightly against her milky white teeth. Her warm, golden eyes no longer glowed with love; they glowed with vengeance. She wasn't the seductress that called him *d*◈. No, he didn't know who this woman was—this demoness.

Meyana stepped toward him and slowly climbed on top of him, straddling him as he used to be so fond of. Michael growled low in his throat, and his teeth elongated simultaneously. He was furious at this betrayal of his trust and affection. As she sat on him, she leaned forward, reaching over his head and pulling a silver, serrated knife out from within the headboard. Michael went still, knowing she was the one with control in this situation.

"Why?" His voice was filled with rage and devastation.

She leaned down and put her lips to his ear. "Because you are a vampire, *d*◈, and I must do what I have promised—what I was *born* to do."

She leaned back and placed a kiss on his mouth, lingering for the smallest of moments. He did not kiss her back but simply watched her. "I'm sorry, Michael, but it was not meant to be." With both hands wrapped around the hilt, she raised the knife over her head, as if he was to be her sacrifice. She took aim, preparing to strike down into his heart hard and fast.

Before she could, though, something struck out at her and knocked her over. She caught herself with her left hand and, snarling, Meyana looked to her right.

A demon had come.

Standing nearly seven feet tall, the demon was in a towering humanoid form—with hairless and wrinkled, gray skin like a decaying corpse. Its eyes were burning red like molten lava, its ears oversized and pointed. A tail roughly 9 feet in length whipped behind it, a razor-sharp spear-tip adorning the end and ready to slice through flesh and bone. The demon smiled, and multiple rows of needle-like teeth made their entrance to the party.

In a panic, Meyana tried to cast a spell to disarm the demon. Vines and roots grew rapidly around the demon's feet as she attempted to entangle it. However, it merely stepped through them, its flesh searing each strand and leaf. Each new one that popped up, the demon stomped on it with six-toed feet, each bearing two backward-facing talons. Unleashing a roar, the vines and roots shriveled in response. While his enchantress was distracted, Michael freed himself from his bindings and retreated from the bed to stand next to the demon.

"No!" she exclaimed. Despite her anger, he thought he could hear fear in her voice as well.

She shut her eyes and began casting furiously, her voice growing louder and louder as she called upon her powers to unleash the ground beneath their feet. The earth began to rumble, the house shaking violently and dressers toppling over. The ceiling began to crumble, and the floor began to break apart where Michael stood. He glanced at the demon, snarling in response as it released its own growl, and together they faced the SpellCaster.

All of a sudden, with Meyana fully entranced and the house crumbling around them, the spell that had bound Michael to her was broken. It was as if a blindfold had been removed: the magic was ripped from his soul, and he was free. Whatever hold she had over him was gone, and he remembered everything: his ability to enter dreams, porting, calling forth demons—all of it.

Most importantly, he remembered *Celie*.

Oh my god... What have I done?

Howling with a wrath born of vengeance, Michael sped across the room. He hauled Meyana close and lifted her off the floor with her arms pinned to her sides. Unable to cast, her eyes grew wide as she met his stormy gray stare; all shaking and rumbling of the house ceased. Michael tilted his head back and roared Celie's name, his anguish and rage filling the air, and as she heard the emotions issue forth from his ragged heart, Meyana knew her life was over.

He brought her in close. "Death is too good for you," he seethed sharply, violence dripping from every word.

Before she could bargain, he lunged at her throat, ripping it out with a ferocity he hadn't felt in decades. He tore into her flesh, his teeth hitting bone, and seized upon her blood, drinking his fill of her as recompense for her transgressions. It was spicy and intoxicating, leaving him feeling drunk with power.

"*D◈*..." Her voice was barely audible as she made one last attempt to seduce him.

As he drained her, she lost the ability to stand and fell. He caught her in his arms and continued to drink from her. Soon she was nothing more than a shell of the goddess she had once been, a beautiful husk of dried flesh and fragile bone.

Ferocious and angry, Michael threw her corpse away and spun around. His eyes met the demon's, daring it to take advantage of the frenzied situation. Without hesitating, the demon lowered its head and bowed, evaporating into nothing.

Michael fell to his knees, his head hanging low. His hair was disheveled, half of it having come separated from his ponytail and hiding his face in shadow. A single tear fell from his right eye, dropping onto his hand. As if triggering his release, his head suddenly flew back, and a demonic wail left him. He cried out for all he had lost—all that had been taken from him. His deafening roar eventually faded, and he was left with nothing but silence and an unbearable ache for Celie—for his love.

After some time had passed, Michael stormed through the house, searching for memories and anything of Celie's. The house had been emptied of everything that had been theirs—had been *hers*—all traces of her existence were gone. Despite living with him these past several months, it was as if she had never been there at all: she might as well have been a ghost.

After searching everywhere, he realized the only thing left of her were his memories—and the ring he had intended to give her.

Michael found where Meyana had hidden a phone in a dresser drawer. Of course, she had done so in Celie's old room. He hadn't been in there since the SpellCasters had attacked them. He immediately dialed Xander.

"Where the hell have you been, man! You two were supposed to come camping with me and Kat, and it's like you dropped off the face of the earth. We haven't heard from you in nearly a week, and you just call out of the blue? What the actual—"

"Shut up, Xander!"

In an instant, Xander was in military mode. "What happened? How many were there? Are you still in danger?"

"It's— Fuck, I'm still not sure—"

"Tell me."

"We—we were attacked. Celie..." He choked on her name, shame and anger warring inside of him. "Celie's gone. She's— They fucking took her, Xander."

"Who? Who took her?"

Michael briefed Xander on everything: the SpellCasters, the attack, Celie's disappearance, his mind-wipe—and the seduction of Meyana. "It's indescribable. I had no idea anything was wrong. None.

It was just— Xander, I knew something was missing—I *knew* it. But I couldn't— Nothing was left..." He trailed off.

"Damn right you knew something was missing! *Celie* was missing. You can't replace what you have with her, no matter how good-looking or tempting that bitch was."

"I know, and now I've got to find her. I *need* to find her."

"Kat knows a guy. Ricky is his name: he's an IT genius. I'll get with her, and we'll contact you once we've gotten in touch with him. He can help track down Celie."

"Thanks, friend. I can't— Damnit, Xander—I can't lose her."

"I'm on it."

With that, they hung up, and Michael sat quietly in the dark, waiting for answers—waiting to find her.

Chapter Three

Diamhair

Ireland: home of the Fae, castles, and kings of old.

I was a long way from...where? Hell if I knew. I couldn't remember. I just knew that this wasn't home for me. I was away from things that felt familiar. I was around complete strangers.

I didn't know who I was.

The men and women at the Garda station were very kind to me, asking me all kinds of questions to try to help me. Could I remember anything about where I woke up? Could I remember anything about how I had arrived in *Éire* (Ireland)? What about my clothing—did I have any memory of the *mona* (money) in my pocket? Did I recall what the *sliabh* (mountain) logo meant? Was there any recollection of *mo bhaile* (my home)?

They were obviously concerned for my well-being, but there was only so much they could do. They put me in a beige prison cell for the evening, giving me a simple ham sandwich and tea. It was a pleasantly satisfying meal in a semi-comforting way. I had a warm blanket and squishy pillow, and they gave me a green *seaicéad*, or jacket, from their lost and found. The night I arrived at the station, I eventually went to sleep—mentally confused and afraid, yet physically comfortable and toasty.

The next morning, I was told I would be taken to a local bed and breakfast hosted by a woman named Fiadh Murphy. I hopped into one of the tiny Garda vehicles with one of the young officers behind the wheel. They drove me several miles across green countryside, over paved roads and next to long, stone walls. Eventually the car pulled onto the gravel driveway of the tiniest, lovely cottage on the outskirts of the county. All manner of colorful flowers and vibrant, variegated herbs and bushes lined the property border. A beautiful pasture was next door, complete with several fluffy brown cows, a single pitch-black horse, and two cream-colored ponies. The building itself was a vernacular style: solid white, with a grass green front door and shutters, and a thatched roof. Each end of the cottage was decorated with a gray chimney, gentle smoke coming from one of them.

Altogether, it was adorable.

Standing just outside the front door was a small elderly lady. She wore a deep, marine blue shawl wrapped around a tan dress, with worn, brown mary janes on her tiny feet. A few wisps of her snow white hair blew across her weathered face with the gusty breeze, the rest held back in a french twist. She wore no jewelry, but her face beamed with a welcoming smile, and it was the only adornment she needed. Her cheeks were ruddy and her blue eyes twinkled, accentuated by the color of her wrap.

Needless to say, I fell in love with her immediately.

She called out to me as I exited the vehicle. "Miss?"

"Hello!" I waved to her as I struggled to close the heavy door. Once I did, the Garda barely bid me farewell before they were off down the laneway. They had given me little when I left the station, except to say that Mrs. Murphy had opened her home to me.

"That was a fast exit." I watched the vehicle speed away, then turned to Mrs. Murphy. "Hi there!"

"*Dia dhuit* (Hello), Miss. Welcome to *Teach Páirceanna Glasa*: Green Fields House. How's about ye?"

"Oh, very well, thank you."

"*Go maith* (Good). Come with me."

Enjoying the smell of sweet grass and wildflowers that perfumed the air, I followed Mrs. Murphy into her little cottage. Inside was the smell of baking bread, steeping tea, and honey. Her home was sparsely decorated: a long wooden seat, a wood desk, two small end tables with tiny lamps upon them, and two wooden chairs were about the main room. A lovely, red, hand-woven rug adorned the middle. She led me up a steep flight of stairs to a very bijou room. A patchwork quilt lay draped across a wood frame bed. A small oak dresser stood in a corner with a painted porcelain wash bowl on top. She had laid out pillows and an extra blanket for me. I turned to her and smiled.

"This is lovely. Thank you."

"*Tá fáilte romhat* (You're welcome). Take a moment to freshen up. When you're ready, come downstairs for some *tae* (tea)."

"Oh, absolutely. Thank you again."

She turned and left me there, in this incredibly cute, tiny room, and I sat down on the bed. I looked around, noticing the simple decorations, such as a small blue vase of white and yellow wildflowers on the windowsill and a small St. Brigid's cross over the doorway. I took off my jacket and laid it across the foot of the bed.

Then I began to cry.

I'm not one for pity-parties. At least, I don't remember being that person, but I felt so alone. The generosity of the people here moved me. Everyone was being so kind and selfless, and I couldn't have been more appreciative of it. However, I felt like I was floating in an ocean, singular and infinite, displaced from everything and everyone. The void of my memory was as black as a moonless night with a cloud-covered sky, empty of all that would make me whole. It was as if I had a hole within me, and I wept over it, hoping to fill it to the brim and make it disappear within my sorrow.

After a few minutes of tears, my sadness gave way to my resolve, and I stood up and dusted myself off. I went over to the washing bowl and splashed some cold water on my face, using a small hand towel to pat myself dry. Once I was sure I was collected and my eyes were no longer red, I turned and headed down the stairs to see Mrs. Murphy.

"Mrs. Murphy?"

"In here, dear," came the reply from behind me to the right. I rounded the stairwell and a corner, walking through the main room. In another room behind it was a minuscule kitchen, with a small moss-colored table and two mustard yellow chairs painted with vines and delicate red flowers. Mrs. Murphy sat in one chair and gestured for me to sit in the other across from her. Naturally, I complied.

"I want to immediately start by thanking you, Mrs. Murphy. You can't know how much I appreciate that you've opened your home to me. I will help out in any way I can."

"Of course, Miss. And I'll be holdin' ya ta that. But first, I need ta know what ta be callin' ye. Have ye thought of a name fer yerself?" She watched me with a curiosity that lent her a witchy appearance. It was clear she had never met someone who had forgotten themselves before.

"Um...no? I guess I've been so busy trying to remember my name that I haven't thought of anything in the meantime."

"Americans... Alright. Well t'en. Since ye come from America, let's call ya Meri fer short. Will that sit alright wit ye?"

"Meri..." I tried it out, the name sounding strange on my tongue, but it would do. "I'll take it. Meri it is."

"Alright, Meri. Here's how we operate 'round t'ese parts: mornings are fer feeding the cows and horses. Ye'll also need to muck the stalls fer the horses and brush them. Make sure t'ey have plenty of water and such. In the afternoons, I'll be expectin' ye ta help wit the cooking and baking."

"That's it? Sounds terribly fair." I meant it. It was the least I could do.

"Indeed. We'll start wit t'at and see where we end up."

"Wonderful."

"Tae?" She held up a teapot, offering to pour me a cup. Her table was adorned with a tray of scones and fresh honey in a jar.

"Oh, yes, please."

Mrs. Murphy poured me a cup of delicious tea. She then offered me a small plate with a fresh-baked scone laden with silky, golden honey on it. I ate it with relish, delighting in the comforting tastes that only come from homemade foods. She nodded at my enthusiasm and went about sipping her tea.

What commenced was an amusing conversation. Mrs. Murphy insisted that I call her Fiadh ("Mrs. Murphy was me mother-in-law"). She was also adamant that I continue trying to recover my identity, saying, "You'll never know where yer goin' until ye know where ye been."

I couldn't agree with her more.

"Ye really don't know anyt'ing about yerself?"

"No, ma'am."

"Och, none of this 'ma'am' business."

"Sorry."

"And stop apologizin' for t'ings! You have nothin' ta apologize for."

"Okay, Fiadh."

"I know Patrick (back at the Garda) is going ta be lookin' for people who know ye. But it's up ta ye to keep searchin' yer memories. It's all up here." She tapped the side of her head.

"I try, I do. But it's like it's held hostage behind a locked door, and I don't have the key."

"Keep tryin', dear. Keep tryin.'"

I helped her make some mutton stew for dinner, and then we sat and talked about *Éire*. With the savory smells perfuming the air, she told me stories of having grown up in this land, and I listened and laughed at her colorful tales. It was wonderful to meet someone so seasoned and so full of life.

One story was of a horse that traveled the countryside in search of its master. It met all manner of creatures and people, until it came to a pond. While drinking from the pond, it fell in and turned into a fish. As a fish, it swam the length of the pond until it met another fish just like it. They became fast friends and spent their days lazily circling the pond, jumping into the air, and catching bugs at dawn and dusk.

Then one day, many years later, a wizened old woman came to the pond. In exchange for collecting a jewel at the bottom of the pond, she transformed each fish back into their true forms. The horse discovered the other fish was its true master! They left to travel home together, spending the rest of their days in comfort and joy.

Fiadh's entire life was full of amazing people, joyful insights, and some sad stories. Her husband had died three years before, so she had been all alone since then. Fiadh opened up her home to weary travelers and those who were lost yet found by the Garda. It gave her some company and help around the cottage. But mostly, she did it so she could continue having little adventures since she couldn't leave home like she used to.

"And t'at was how I came to have t'ese five Highland cows."

I laughed and clapped. "That was brilliant. Utterly brilliant."

The night had crept in—slow and quiet—as we talked over tea and candlelight. Crickets were chirping outside, and frogs bellowed just outside the window. The sun had dipped lazily below the horizon some time ago.

Fiadh sighed and slapped her hands on her knees, rising up from her seat. "Well, I'm off ta bed. *Oíche mhaith* (goodnight), Meri." She walked out of the kitchen toward the stairs.

"*Oíche mhaith*, Fiadh," I called after her.

I continued to sip my last cup and sighed. If this was going to be my life, I had the feeling this was a welcome change. Something so unpretentious couldn't possibly be a bad thing for me.

I took my emptied cup and Fiadh's, stood up, and walked over to the sink. Fiadh's cottage had running water, so I washed each cup quickly and set them out to dry, then I headed up the stairs to my room. After washing my face, I changed into a long shift she had left for me and climbed into bed.

My window was open, and I heard the call of an owl just outside. A breeze blew through the window and caressed my skin, chill and crisp. I snuggled deeper under the quilted blanket and turned to my side, grabbing my pillow and pulling it more firmly under my head. I was terribly comfortable.

The beauty of Ireland and the hospitality of its people had me in its grasp. Everything was going amazingly well. I could only imagine what the opposite would have been: no family, no loved ones, no home—not even a name. I still had no idea how I'd arrived here, but I was thankful that I had. Afterall, it could have been much, much worse.

I lay in my bed that second night in *Éire*, staring at the flowers on the windowsill, repeating my new name over and over again. "Meri... Meri..." It was beginning to grow on me. One day I might learn my real name, but until that day came, this was who I was now. Meri No Name, the American at Green Fields House. The strange girl who showed up in Roscommon, Ireland with no memory.

I wondered if anyone was looking for me? I knew the Garda had put out an alert to the other stations. They also submitted something to a contact with Interpol in case anything had come over from the United States. Perhaps I had loved ones trying to find me. I hoped I did.

Until then, I would stay where I was.

The morning brought new adventures.

Fiadh was up bright and early, ready to show me where the feed was, how much to get, and where to take it. I started out just as Fiadh requested; I went to the barn and filled a wheelbarrow with grass and hay for the horses, taking it to a spot along the pasture fence they were familiar with. The black horse whinnied happily for me, and the vanilla ponies snorted in pleasure at their breakfast. I was thrilled when I was able to stroke the velvet of a horse's muzzle and forehead.

For all I knew, it was the first time I had ever been able to do that.

Next were the cows. They were easy to feed and very responsive. I named one of them Willful for pushing his way to the front to take first crack at the grass piles. Despite his long dossan hanging over his eyes, Willful sought me out and nuzzled my hand. The others came over to smell me—the new stranger bringing them food. Eventually the fold dispersed back to the pasture or to their open shelter.

I also learned that Fiadh had a dog—a small, shaggy, black-and-white mutt named Seamus, who loved to herd the cows and playfully run around the horses. The horses tolerated him, but sometimes they chased him mercilessly until he came running back to the cottage. He stayed in the barn, but I made sure he received a welcome breakfast, too.

After mucking the stables and shelter, I cleaned myself up. Fiadh gave me thirty euros to go into town and purchase some clothing. She suggested a local opportunity shop—which I learned was a thrift shop—to get some clothing. She also wanted some basic incidentals from the local grocer, and I was only too happy to oblige.

I headed out on foot. The entire trek was about three miles, so it only took roughly an hour to get there. I went into the opportunity shop first and found a treasure trove of vintage t-shirts and decent jeans. These pieces felt more like my speed, so I picked up three shirts and a pair of pants for about eight euros.

Next, I headed over to the grocer, who happened to have some basic necessities on hand—things like underwear and socks. I grabbed some of those, a hairbrush, and a toothbrush and toothpaste. After grabbing the few items that Fiadh needed, I checked out and packed everything up. Carting my haul in two big bags, I began the hike back to the cottage.

On the road, I stopped to watch some skylarks and egrets in the nearby field. I was only there for a moment when I heard a vehicle pull up behind me, the slow crunch of gravel under its tires sounding incredibly loud against the quiet. I turned around in surprise: the road had very little traffic. The baby blue car that slowed alongside me was older, long and wide, with round headlights. Blood-red taillights that sparkled in the sunlight sat beneath large tail fins, and I stared as it pulled around to stop in front of me. I hadn't seen a vehicle like it before—at least, not that I could remember—and certainly not since I had woken up in Ireland.

I could see three silhouettes in the car, each face hidden by the reflective glare on the windows. The driver's side door opened, and a tall, thin man got out. Tan with salt-and-pepper hair, he turned around, and I was surprised to see how young he looked. Dressed all in gray, he watched me with eyes the color of a stormy sea.

I was struck by how he seemed so familiar...

He closed his door and simply stood there, staring at me. I stared back, uncomfortable in the silence but unsure what to do. The bags I carried seemed to grow heavier every second I stood there.

Eventually, he spoke.

"How are you?" He sounded different than the locals: more polished, more enunciated. His dialect wasn't Irish or American like mine.

I paused for a moment—unsure if I should reply or not—before responding with, "I...I'm fine. Thank you."

The man continued to watch me, his face blank and devoid of expression or emotion. It was extremely unsettling. *Who is this guy?*

I blinked several times. "I'm sorry, but— Do we know each other?"

"That depends, *daanav* (demon). Do you know who I am?"

I looked him over again once more, head to toe, but I couldn't place him. "I... I don't think I do...?"

"Ah." He finally smiled, closed-lipped, nearly transforming himself into someone trustworthy. Nearly. I couldn't ignore the fact his smile fell short of his eyes. I could tell he was forcing himself to be pleasant. "Then clearly we do *not* know each other."

"Oh..." I whispered. "Okay."

He tilted his head toward the sun. "'Tis a beautiful day, is it not?"

"Uh, yeah?"

"The birds must agree. They are flying high on the winds today."

I said nothing: I was unable to look away from him. In a moment, I cringed as his smile dropped again. He was back to that same damned blank stare.

He tapped his hand against his side. I would have sworn to you the man was trying to peer right into my very core. Goosebumps flushed my skin and I shivered; the distinct sensation of someone walking over my grave filled me with dread. He smiled again, only this time he showed his teeth: white and polished, his canines wickedly pointed. I shivered again.

"So nice to have seen you. Do have a pleasant day, Miss." He made a small bowing gesture, then his smile was gone. I watched as he climbed back into the vehicle. Starting up the car, he swiftly drove off, kicking up several stones on the way. As the car disappeared into the distance, the sparkling taillights faded away in the daylight.

I never did see who else was in the vehicle.

Immediately, I hustled my way back to the cottage, jogging even, completely unnerved by the encounter. That man had been disturbing—frightening, even. I didn't lie when I told him that I didn't think I knew him; I truly didn't. Still, he was definitely lying to me. Whoever he was, he knew me. There was one other thing for certain based on our little chat: I didn't want to know him.

Chapter Four

Lost and Found

"She's what!"

"Missing, Kat. Celie is missing."

"Oh my god. We've gotta find her! When was the last time he saw her?"

"Roughly a week or so ago."

"Where?"

"The house." Xander was doing his best to keep Kat calm by keeping his own responses chill and smooth. He was used to her getting wound up and dramatic, but this time he understood her feelings far too well: concern was etched on his own face.

"Okay, so we start there. Are there any clues? Does he know if someone took her?"

"No clues except that it was SpellCasters. They sent her somewhere."

"SpellCasters? What the hell are 'SpellCasters'? Witches? Wizards? That kind of thing?"

"Sounds like it to me."

"But I thought witches were all 'harm none'?"

"Not all of them, I guess."

"Well, they were when I was going to circles."

"Say what?"

Kat was pacing back and forth in her apartment. Her dark blonde hair had grown out to just below her chin, and she was repeatedly pushing it back behind her ears. She had three pairs of sparkling diamond studs in each ear but was dressed down in a purple t-shirt and black leggings, with white socks on her feet. She glanced up at Xander: he was seated on her couch, leaning back as if he didn't have a care in the world. His golden eyes were narrowed as he stared at her, expectant of more information.

She stopped mid-pacing to glare at him in incredulity. "How can you just sit there and be so chill? Like, are you immune to this whole thing?"

"Why didn't you tell me you practiced Wicca?"

Kat waved her hand dismissively. "I can't tell you *everything*. We've gotta have some mystery in the relationship, right?"

Xander smirked and reached out to grab her about the waist. Pulling her to sit on his lap, he leaned in and pressed a kiss to her lips. Kat held him close, her hands on the sides of his face. She melted against him as he squeezed her hips. After a moment, she pulled away and touched her forehead to his, eyes closed. She sighed.

"I'm sorry. I don't mean to be like this. I'm just so worried about her."

"I know, baby."

"Who knows where she is, or what kind of place she's stuck in? Is she safe? Is she hurt? We don't know, and it scares the shit out of me." Kat made a growling sound, venting her frustration. "Ugh, this sucks!" She tilted her head back, and Xander began rubbing her back.

"I know this is freakin' you out, Kat, but I'm sure it'll be fine."

"And that crap with Michael? Oh my God. I could kill him!"

"They cast something over him—some kind of curse or magic fog over him. He had *no* idea what was going on or what he was doin' with that female."

"Still. He *cheated* on her! The slime—the sheer and utter slime..." Kat seethed in anger.

Xander sighed. He understood magic was at work, but it was a magic none of them understood. He also knew Kat wasn't going to let Michael's actions go for quite some time. If she was this upset, lord help Michael whenever Celie got her hands on him.

Xander leaned forward to whisper in her ear. "You're getting worked up again." He placed a kiss on her ear lobe, causing her to relax without thinking. Pulling back, he gave her a winsome smile. "Before we do anything else, I need you to breathe, baby. Just breathe for me."

Kat stared into his eyes and took several slow, deep breaths.

"Now, I told Michael that I thought you could talk to your buddy Ricky. He might be able to help locate Celie, right? That would be something more than we have right now."

"Ricky?" She was a little confused before her memory kicked in and lit up her face. "Oh, Ricky! Yes! That's a great idea. Let me call him up and see if he can't help."

Without leaving her perch, Kat angled herself back from Xander towards the coffee table and grabbed her cell phone. She quickly maneuvered to her contact list and found Ricky's number. She pressed the phone symbol, and he answered after just one ring.

"Hello, Katie-kat! How's it hangin'?"

Xander rolled his eyes, clearly unimpressed.

His voice was young, and so was he. Ricky Yun was an acquaintance of Kat's from college. When she was 22 years-old, Ricky was 16. His family left South Korea when he was still very little, but they pushed him through school at a fast pace, and his brilliant mind was able to keep up with just about anything. Now he was a top-level computer forensic scientist and in demand by numerous top companies. He worked as a consultant, going where the work was and making his own schedule. He had made millions, all before he was even 20.

"Hiya, Ricky! Low and slow, as always." She winked at Xander.

"Oh yeah? What's going on? I haven't heard from you in a while. Thought you dropped off the face of the earth or somethin'?"

"Long story, sweetie. But listen, I could use your help; it's urgent. Are you in the middle of anything?"

"Not at the moment. What's up?"

"My friend has gone missing. Do you remember Celie?"

"Red? Sure, I remember her. She's missing?"

"Yeah. For a few days now."

"Have you reported it to the police? I know the movies say to wait 48 hours, but in real life they don't actually expect you to do that, you know?"

Kat snorted. "No. I don't think the police are really the right people for this."

"Um... Okay...?"

"Let's just say that the police would really muck up the situation."

"Interesting... Okay, shoot: what do you need from me?"

"Here's the thing: I was hoping you could work your magic and search the interwebs for any sign of her? Like maybe someone reported finding her, or she's for sale somewhere? Something like that? Not saying she's been trafficked or anything: I'm just wondering if you can see if anyone found her?"

"I see..." Ricky went quiet.

Afraid she had upset him with her request, Kat began to ramble, words flying at lightning speed. "I mean, you don't have to. I get that I haven't talked to you in a while, and this probably seems like I'm only calling you for a favor and not to catch up or something. And—" She sighed. "—you'd be right. I just really need help to find her, and you're the best person I know who can help me figure this out. I can probably make it up to you—like tickets to something or a night out on the town? I'm sure I have a friend or two that would be perfect for you, if you are looking for a date. But I really, really need your help, Ricky. I'm just hoping you'll jump in any time here and get me to shut up before I say or do something that totally ruins my chances of you working your magic. I probably already put my foot in my mouth, but then again, I do that, so just tell me to shut up now, Ricky."

Silence.

"Ricky?"

Still nothing.

"Hello?"

"I'm here. Calm your tits, Katie-kat. I found her."

"Holy Jesus! That's amazing!"

"Yeah. While you were blabbering on—which was super impressive by the way, and I'm definitely taking you up on your offer—I ran some basics through a database or two. Looks like she's in Ireland."

"Ire— Are you effing kidding me? How in the—wait, never mind. What else does it say? Is she okay?" She froze. "Is—is she alive?"

Xander, who had been looking at his own phone, perked up and swung a wide-eyed face to stare at Kat. Kat mouthed, 'This is insane.'

"The police there reported her turning up in Ross Common—"

"*Roscommon?*"

"Oh, you know it?"

"Get the eff outta here! My grandmother's family is from there! How bizarre is this shit?"

"You can say that again."

"Does it say if she's okay? Is she hurt? Where is she staying? You mentioned the police: was she arrested?"

"Slow...down..." Ricky drew out each word, laughing.

"Sorry! Just tell me if she's alright?" Kat was bouncing up and down in barely contained excitement. Xander held on to her waist and simply raised an eyebrow.

"She's great—I think."

"You think?"

"Uh... Reading, reading, reading... Oh—oh, that's not good."

"What?"

"Well, the police report— It says— Crap, how do I put this..."

"Just spit it the hell out, Ricky."

Ricky's barely contained concern came through in his voice. "Celie's got amnesia."

"What!"

"Yeah, she couldn't tell them anything about herself. All they could figure out is that she's American, and they can't hold her for being a foreigner, so they put her up with a local Irish woman until someone came forward or they found out more info."

"Shit, you're right. This is bad." Kat's brow furrowed in consternation. Xander nudged her for more info, but she held up a hand to shush him. He huffed and crossed his well-muscled arms.

"It could be worse, though. At least we know she's alive."

"Oh, for sure! Oh my god, okay—okay okay. Thank you so so much, Ricky! I need to make some calls and schedule some flights."

"Do you need any help getting those set up? I can just—"

"No, we can manage but thank you! Can I call you later after I get back?"

"Sure thing, shorty. No worries."

"You're awesome."

"I know it."

"Thanks, Ricky."

"I got you. Later, girl."

Kat made sure the call was disconnected and turned to Xander. She took in a deep breath and exhaled slowly, trying to calm herself down. Her eyes were still wide, her facial expressions a war of excitement, anxiety, and confusion. "Okay. I'm gonna tell you everything, but we have a huge problem."

"Which is?"

"Which one of us is going to tell Michael she has amnesia?"

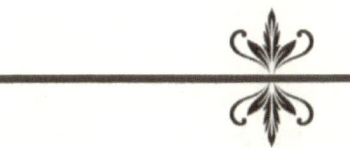

Five hours later, the three of them were squished together in coach on an international flight to Dublin. The seats were funky, squeaky pleather, and barely big enough to fit Michael and Xander's large, imposing frames. Despite the ease of getting a first-class flight, they wanted to keep a low profile, unsure where or when the SpellCasters might strike again. So cramped quarters it was, with stinky seats and screaming children, as the plane took off.

The stewardess came by and offered them each a drink, which they gladly took: a whiskey for Michael, a bourbon for Xander, and a vodka for Kat. Ice tinkled as each glass was handed over. Once they were settled, the three of them talked about how best to tackle their first meeting with Celie.

Needless to say, arguments ensued and got a little out of hand.

"She's not gonna remember you." Kat was exasperated with Michael's romantic nonsense. "Try and get that through your thick skull."

"Kat's right, man." Xander was used to this level of frustration from Kat, but Michael was being beyond bullheaded and stubborn. "According to the police, she doesn't even remember *herself.* There's no way she's gonna know who you are."

"I know she doesn't remember who she is: I've read the report. But *you* need to understand that she and I have a connection." Michael was tired of repeating himself. He stared down into his drink. "I have to believe it. I'm sure I can get through to her—that our connection will help...I don't know—wake her up?"

Kat leaned around Xander to glare at him, sneering, "It didn't help out when you were in bed with She-Slut, Queen of the Sex Jungle, now did it?" She was still reeling from that news and feeling very protective of Celie.

"Fuck you, too." He was still angry at himself—ashamed of what happened and what he'd done—and he didn't need the condescension coming from Kat, too. He had betrayed Celie with that Spellcaster bitch, and even killing her couldn't make up for what he'd done. He was going to do everything he could to prove his love for Celie—even if it meant sacrificing himself to protect her; she was worth it to him.

Michael just needed to get her back—*if* he could get her back...

"Hey, hey, hey." Xander threw his hands up in an attempt to separate them. "Everyone just calm down. I'm gonna need you both to put this aside and work together." He glanced at Kat, then Michael, then back to Kat. "If we can't do that, we might as well just leave Celie in Ireland for good."

Kat sat back in her seat, tears in her eyes. "Oh god, you're right." She leaned forward again. "I'm sorry, Michael. I'm just so damn angry! And *you're* here, but the SpellCasters *aren't*... It was just easier to make you my target." Her face scrunched up in anger again. "I can't wait to find them and ram their spell shit right up their asses."

"I'm sorry, too, Kat." Michael paused for a moment. "You know, I don't know if I ever thanked the two of you for finding her." He turned to look them both in the eye. "It means the world to me. Thank you."

Xander spoke first, smiling at his old friend. "Don't mention it: we're happy to help out. I can't imagine what she's going through over there: strange country, strange people..."

"Strange body..." Both men looked at Kat. "Remember, she doesn't know who she is." Kat firmly believed she was the realist in this bunch.

"Right..."

Michael took a swig of his whiskey and set down the glass on the open tray table in front of Xander. "If she doesn't remember me–"

"She won't," interjected Kat.

"—then I'm going to do whatever I have to in order to win her back." His hand was on the edge of his armrest, and his knuckles went white as he tightened his grip. "I'm not coming home without her." He turned toward both of them in his seat. "I need you both to help me: help me get her to remember. Stories, songs, food: if there's anything that might trigger her, we need to use it."

Kat smiled at Xander, then looked over at Michael. "Not a problem. I've known her my entire life. I've got plenty of stories."

"I'm sure I can think of a few." To Xander, it felt like a lifetime had passed since their exploits with the cult. No way would he let Celie forget why they were friends.

"Even if it's something negative, it could still bring back her memory." Michael thought about the moment Celie had learned who her father was. It had nearly broken her, but she was strong and came back more powerful than before.

Hell, she even killed the bastard.

Then Michael remembered what they needed to really discuss—what had made him turn white before they boarded the plane. "We need to talk about the elephant in the room. There's one more thing I'm concerned about." They both looked at him expectantly. "She hasn't been feeding."

Kat eyed him suspiciously. "It's only been a week, right? Humans can go up to a month or so."

"But she's not human—not anymore. Look, if she doesn't know *what* she is, and she goes too long without drinking, it can be dangerous—for her and for anyone around her."

"That's a thing?" Kat's face had concern written all over it. "She could...hurt someone?"

"Yes."

Xander's background kicked in, his concern now for the well-being of the people of Roscommon. "Do we have time to take care of this before it's a problem? And what happens if we *don't* get to her?"

Michael glanced at him. "We don't have long—ten, twelve days from her last drink. It's already been *eight*. If we can't get her to remember or get her to feed soon, she's going to turn feral."

"Feral?" Xander was unsure if he wanted to hear more. He was already picturing Celie turning into a hulking monster, with razor-sharp claws shredding through the night air.

"It'll start with difficulty going out during the day. She'll feel sluggish, have intense headaches, light sensitivity... Cravings will start, but for something she won't recognize, and she'll want to eat all the time. Before long, it will progress into only wanting raw meat."

"Like steak tartare?" Kat's voice had dropped to a whisper.

"If by steak tartare you mean people, then yes."

"Oh my god..." Sheer horror was written all over her face.

"That settles it." Xander slammed his hand down on the arm of the chair. "We need to get her memory back ASAP."

Kat agreed. "Right. Like I said, I don't think she'll remember you, but your vampy stuff might be the right trigger."

Michael stared at the back of the seat in front of him for a minute, lost in thought. The idea of Celie going feral was not one that he was happy about. He had thought about that when he first used his abilities on her to send her home, concerned that he would have to intervene then. But she had found him, broken through his abilities and come to their home. *Their home.* To have this all coming back up now, after they had spent so much time together, such blissful time... The thought was enough to send him reeling.

Michael blinked and turned his head. "Vampy stuff?" He'd only heard part of her statement.

"Blood, talking in her head, et cetera—you know, that vampy thing that you do so well..." She used some old vernacular to get him on the same page.

"Oh, right." He shook his head. "Sorry. I'm just so distracted by my own thoughts. I keep thinking of her by herself over there. I also keep thinking of the abilities she has, if any of that has come into play yet."

Kat had only recently learned of Celie's ghostly abilities. "For real. Can you imagine all the spirits over there? She could manifest the whole damn country with the history they have over there!"

"We'll be there in no time, man." Xander smacked Michael on the arm. "You'll see. This flight will go by faster than you think."

Michael nodded and leaned back into his seat. "I hope so."

He listened to Kat and Xander begin to talk about her family in Ireland, listened to the sound of their hearts beating for each other, and he closed his eyes. Thank God he'd fed before they traveled. He struggled to drown out the sounds on the plane, of chatter and beverage carts, of crying children and exalted conversations, of pulsating blood. He singled his focus on the coming days, on their mission, on Celie.

Oh Celie... What have I done... I'm going to fix this. I'm going to bring you back to me.

Michael vowed that he would get Celie back. He would get her memory restored and make up to her all the horrible things he'd done. Then they would be together, and they could fight the SpellCasters, banishing them into oblivion. He was confident he could do it, that their love would be the key to breaking whatever had been cast over her. He only hoped he could get there in time...

Chapter Five

Tús

I had been in Ireland for just over a week when I began getting nasty, nauseating headaches.

"Willful, stop pushing everyone. You'll get your food; don't worry."

I was feeding the cows on an especially peaceful, early morning. The sun was just peeking through the trees on the far side of the pasture. The golden glow pierced the branches and highlighted the forest silhouette. Above, the sky was a lavender blue with fluffy clouds made from fading orange and raspberry sorbet. The moon still hung overhead, a crescent of dimming brilliance. The smell of sweet grass and the animals hung in the air, and I took a deep breath. This had to be a version of heaven.

Suddenly, sharp, splintering pain was stabbing me in the back of my head. I bent forward, clapping my hands to my temples and dropping the bucket I carried to the ground. Grimacing as the shards of agony ripped my head clean in two, I inhaled sharply and grit my teeth.

Yet, just as suddenly as it had begun, the pain ended. I blinked, once then twice, slowly standing upright again. I stood still for a moment, anticipation of a repeat pain performance freezing me in place, but eventually I relaxed as it failed to surface.

I looked around at the cows, who were chewing and staring at me thoughtfully. "Nothing to see here, folks." Then I bent down and retrieved my bucket, mindful to stand up slowly once again for fear of agitating the unknown issue.

Oddly enough, I had a sudden craving for a large, juicy steak.

I flinched at the thought, surrounded by fluffy highland cows that acted like over-large dogs. *I couldn't possibly eat my friends.* I had been doing fine without eating much meat while staying with Fiadh. Perhaps I had been a vegetarian during my previous life?

Yet the craving remained, and I found myself salivating at the thought of a medium rare, crosshatch grilled piece of meat. Delicious images of juices pouring down my throat permeated my imagination. The taste of salty meat seemed a moment away from my tongue, and I swallowed instinctively.

Shaking my head to avail it of these intense thoughts, I was determined to focus on my tasks. I gripped the bucket handle tightly and marched back to the barn, stopping only once to pet Seamus and give him a scratch under his soft chin. Once inside, the bucket was put away, then I walked back outside and turned toward the house.

As I reached for the front doorknob, another sharp headache split my head in half, leaving me reeling. I fell over as the sound of Fiadh calling out to me rang in my ears, her voice echoing sharply like clanging bells, bouncing back and forth down my ear canal and into my brain. I sat up and leaned to the left, vomiting profusely, feeling that impossibly frightening sensation of being unable to breathe as I retched violently and incessantly. Fear gripped me as I struggled to bring air into my lungs.

Like before, the headache stopped suddenly. The lack of ringing in my ears was a deafening silence as I blinked, looking around the drive and across the fields. Flinching slightly at the sensation, I felt the diminutive hand of Fiadh on my shoulder. I glanced up at her.

"Ya wee girl, what's taken wit ye?" Concern was etched across her wrinkled face.

"I...I don't know..." I looked back down at my hands, shaking. "It must have been something I ate?"

"I doubt that. We'll get the *dochtúir* to come out for ye."

"Oh no, we don't need to do that, Fiadh. I'll be fine. I just need some rest."

Fiadh looked at me sharply and clicked her tongue. "Ye'll be seein' the doctúir or my name isn't Fiadh Murphy. Now come wit me, lass." Despite her size and age, she helped me stand up.

I looked down at her, towering over her as she frowned at me. I couldn't help but feel so much warmth and caring for her. She had no reason to be so concerned about me, but she was. I felt loved by this tiny woman, and it melted my heart.

"Okay, okay. I'll see the doctor."

"Darn right ye will, *cailín amaideach*."

I laughed. "Oh, lord love you, Fiadh."

Fiadh escorted me into the house and up the steps to the bedroom. I went to sleep. Roughly two hours later, the doctor came and examined me, finding nothing wrong with me but that my blood pressure was elevated. He prescribed me with a common blood pressure medicine and told me to stay in bed the rest of the day. Fiadh wouldn't let me rebuttal that last bit and headed outside to finish taking care of the beasties of the field. I heard the ponies whinnie through my bedroom window.

While Fiadh was outside, I felt hungry, so I quietly crept downstairs and into the kitchen. I opened the icebox and took a look at what she had available. Spying a beef roast, I proceeded to hack into and ravage it. The flavor touched my tongue, saliva running down my throat, and I sighed in satisfaction.

After a few minutes of this, I paused. Why was I so fixated on this? I hadn't eaten beef since I had arrived in Ireland, let alone something so rare as this roast.

I finished the piece I was eating and closed the icebox. I rinsed my hands and then went back upstairs to bed. Sliding under the covers of the quilt, I lay still and quiet.

Something was wrong. I didn't know what it was, but I knew something was happening to me. Headaches, elevated blood pressure, cravings for meat... What could this all mean?

I focused on the sounds coming from the green fields outside, letting the larks lull me to sleep. Dreams of fire permeated my night. Nightmares of lost love woke me, and I choked on a scream. Eventually I went back to sleep, but I felt in my bones that something bad was coming.

The next day, I felt the sunshine warm my skin as I went outside. The heat of it melted away my fears from the night before. Rays of light cast a golden glow across the fields and plastered a smile on my face.

I needed some personal comfort, so I spent some time in the barn with Seamus. He subsisted on belly rubs, various scratches, and some bits of bacon from the morning breakfast. Having a pet is something truly amazing. They are so unconditionally loving and devoted, asking for nothing in return except the things that we all need to survive: food, water, shelter, and companionship. I could find no reason but to love pets equally, understanding that they cannot speak, but their actions do so loudly. Seamus was no exception, and I showered him with affection.

SPELLCAST FROM DARKNESS

After spending some time in the barn, I decided to head into town. I thought a walk in the warm sun and a change of scenery would do me some good. I bid Fiadh farewell and headed towards Roscommon.

Upon my arrival, I went to The Square and then over to Castle Street, each brimming with pubs. There were small ones, big ones, ones that offered flashy drinks, and ones that afforded a uniquely old world experience. I picked one of the latter, named *Madra Agus Caróg*, and went inside, determined to have a drink now that it was after noon.

The darkness was welcoming, as the light outside had begun to sting my eyes. The interior was brimming with dark green and stained oak trim. The floor was made from stained oak as well, and the walls were adorned with antiques from old battles, kitchens, and blue-collar work. Harps and tin whistles were strategically placed alongside song lyrics, and there was a small stage in the back for local performers. The oak bar lined one side of the long room, and behind it was a long mirror adorned with numerous whiskeys, scotches, bourbons, vodkas, and other types of liquors and libations. Small clear glasses were placed here and there for easy access by the bartender.

I felt the rush of the cold interior as the solid door closed behind me. The bartender, an older woman with sandy blonde hair pulled back in a ponytail, glanced up at me and went back to drying a glass. Several people were sitting at tables here and there, so I chose to sit at the bar. I pulled out a stool, and the feet made a squealing noise as it slid across the floor. A few faces glanced up at me, making me squirm a bit inside as I climbed onto the stool. Once I was in place, the bartender came over.

"What'll you have?" She was terse and definitely not in the mood for chit-chat.

I paused for a moment, then spoke with confidence. "A whiskey."

An eyebrow went up, then the bartender turned and walked away to pour me a serious Irish whiskey. I have no idea what label it was, but when she returned, I knew it was potent based on the smell of it.

I coughed a little as the bartender watched me. Whatever it was must have had a high-octane rating because the fumes burned my nose hairs.

The bartender walked back to the other end of the bar after she placed my drink in front of me. Staring from down the other end, the bartender kept an eye on me, waiting to see how I managed my drink. Taking my chances, I said the hell with it and tipped back the glass to down my whiskey. Boy did that burn a hole in my throat. I stifled a cough and inhaled sharply, swallowing past the burn.

Setting the glass down on the bar, I tapped it twice on the wood. That startled me. I couldn't recall why it struck me to do that. It was almost instinctual. After a moment, I raised my hand to signal the bartender and asked for another one. She smiled at me and winked this time.

After my second whiskey, I sat and contemplated my existence. Isn't that what we all do when we get in our cups? I wasn't exactly there yet, but it seemed right, in this bar in Roscommon, Ireland, to think about...well, all of it. Who was I? Where was I from? Where was I headed? What happened to me? Did I have a purpose? Why was I here in Ireland?

I still had no clues or information from the Garda about how I wound up in the country. It seemed unique that an American would just pop up in the middle of a country with no history or memory. Had I been with people that died? Had I been with someone that abandoned me? No one had claimed me. Was I an orphan? Maybe I wasn't missed?

But that still didn't explain how not even an employer sought me out. Maybe I was unemployed? But how could I be in Ireland without a VISA? It was all so confusing and made my brain hurt.

Out of the corner of my eye, I saw a figure approach the bar on my right. They were large, with a masculine frame. As soon as I looked at them, they glanced at me and then disappeared. I flinched.

The figure had been transparent.

What in the hell just happened? I shook it off and stared down into my glass. *It must be the whiskey.* Whew. This Irish stuff definitely packed a punch!

After spending a decent amount of time at the pub, I went to take my leave. I thanked the bartender for her kindness to a stranger and left a decent tip with the funds Fiadh had given me to go exploring with. I hopped off the stool, glanced to my right, and shook my head again. That figure definitely had been a figment of my imagination.

As I walked out the door, I brushed past someone. It was a man. An attractive man. A *delicious* man. He smelled of wood and spices, and it was heavenly.

"Excuse me." I inhaled his scent, taking in several breaths as I passed him.

"My apologies." He touched my arm, and then our eyes met. His cool, steel gray eyes went wide, and his breath caught. He froze. "Celie?" He said the name with the most hushed voice. "Celie? Oh my god, is it really you?"

I jumped, anxious and frightened. I was aroused at the notion that he might know me. He sounded like he did, but I didn't know myself. Who was this man? I mean, he was incredibly handsome, with strong features, rich cheekbones, and soft full lips. His mahogany-colored hair was pulled back in a low ponytail. He wore a brown leather jacket with a blue t-shirt and jeans, brown boots on his feet. His hand on my arm was warm, the grip solid and growing tighter with every breath. I felt intimidated, surprised, and definitely caught off guard.

"Celie?"

I was going to be careful and cautious about this. I wasn't getting a negative vibe about him, but his awareness of me had me on edge. After nine days of nothing, it was alarming to have someone who *wasn't* Garda coming up to me and acknowledging me in such a way. My palms began to sweat.

"Celie, it's me. It's Michael." His eyes bore into mine. "Please. For the love of God, please tell me you remember me." The urgency in his voice pulled at me, but he wasn't familiar to me in the slightest.

"I'm sorry." I quickly pulled my arm back from his grip. He inhaled sharply. "I...I don't know you." The sorrow in his eyes gave me pause. "But you think you know me? Really?"

He blinked. "Yes. Yes, I do." He turned and motioned to two people who were standing just off the curbside. A man and a woman. Michael ushered me awkwardly away from the door, and they rushed over to where we were.

The woman was vibrant, adorable. Her bright blonde hair was just below her chin and her lips were painted in a beautiful berry red that accentuated her pale skin and bright cheeks. Her black pants were covered mostly by a long tan trench coat wrapped tightly at the waist. Her feet were in black heels. She began talking first. "Oh my god, Celie! Where have you been? We've been frantically looking for you! Of all the places to land, you wound up here. It's amazing! Do you know I have family here? Wow."

The man was talking at the same time. "Thank God we found you! Are you hurt? How are you feeling? Where are you staying? Good god, we've been going crazy trying to find you!" He was a stark contrast to the woman, with silky chocolate skin and a shaved head. His goatee was neat around his full lips. He wore a black t-shirt with dark blue jeans and black boots. Golden eyes peered into mine.

While they peppered me with questions, Michael simply stared at me. I felt his eyes boring deep into me. I could see his hand reach for me, but he stopped and flexed it into a clenched fist. Something was amiss here. I looked up at his face and his lips were pursed, his brow furrowed. I furrowed my own as I narrowed my eyes at him, watching him. He looked away toward the man and woman.

I couldn't place what was wrong. I didn't recognize any of these people, but they seemed terribly concerned for me. I held my hands up to stop them from speaking. Once they did, I stated as clearly as I could that I didn't know them. The woman was especially upset and began to cry.

"No! You can't *not* remember me, Celie!"

"I'm sorry, but I don't."

Her partner sighed. "We hoped you would remember us, but truth be told, we didn't really expect you to." He looked at the woman and smiled softly.

"Again, I'm very sorry," I replied. "Have...have you been to see the Garda?"

"The Garda?"

"The local police," I said. He nodded in understanding. "They have my information, so if I really am this person, you think I am, they can tell you more." I paused. "I just... I don't feel comfortable..."

The woman continued to cry.

"We understand. We'll go visit them now." He turned to the woman and said, "C'mon Kat. The sooner we visit the Garda, the sooner we can start putting things right."

The woman, Kat, sniffled and took his hand. They started to walk away, heading north to the Garda station, and the man stopped, looking back. "Are you coming, Mike?"

I glanced over at Michael. He was staring at me, an expression I still struggle to describe etched into his face. There was longing, sadness, hope, and fear, each one taking a moment to overwhelm his features; his solemn gray eyes said most of it. Again, I caught him stopping himself as he attempted to reach for me. I blinked, and he lowered his eyes. He turned and began to walk toward the man and woman.

Before he took more than two steps, he turned back to look at me. "I'm so sorry, Celie. I'll make this right. I promise." Then he turned back to his friends, and they slowly walked down the street together.

I stood there, staring after them. After they disappeared around the bend, I turned and headed back home to *Teach Páirceanna Glasa*.

On the walk, I couldn't focus. The light of the afternoon sun seemed too bright. There was a glimmer of a headache starting again, and I desperately wanted a rare steak with a fresh-baked potato to soak up some of that whiskey. Served me right for thinking I could tackle that alcohol on an empty stomach.

Most importantly, three strangers could be holding the clue to who I was.

Celie. I might be named Celie. Not Meri, which I had begun to grow accustomed to, but Celie. It was overwhelming.

Once I arrived home, I went to tell Fiadh what happened. Upon arrival, I walked in the front door and found Fiadh in the sitting room with a cup of tea. She had a visitor. A man. I looked at him and noticed something about him wasn't...normal.

"Hi Fiadh. Um, I'm sorry, I didn't know you had company?"

"Och, no worries, lass. This is Connor."

"Connor?"

The man looked at me and smiled. It was then that I noticed that I could see the cabinet behind him—*through him.*

"My husband." Fiadh looked into his eyes and smiled with a happiness I hadn't seen on her face until that very moment.

Then I remembered her telling me Connor had passed away three years ago. I felt my vision pinpoint into darkness. I fainted.

Ionsáiteán

Direction

Rusalka pouted.

"I don't understand why we can't just kill her." Her whining was like a dagger in Brigit's ear.

Brigit sighed loudly. "I've told you, you daft git, we can't kill her because it's more fun watching them go out of control."

"But she'll kill someone. I just know it."

"Says you."

"Says the history!" Rusalka whined louder than before. "That's what always happens. We wipe their memories and then they turn into those beastly creatures! There is always a mess to clean up!"

"Oh, calm down."

"You calm down."

"*Shaanti!* Both of you calm down." Pavan had a map of Ireland laid out on the ground, a scrying board sitting overop of it. He was sitting quietly, questioning with a smoky quartz pendulum. "Please be silent. I'm trying to gauge how much time we have left before we have to act."

The girls were silent as their partner scried and queried, the pendulum swinging to and fro, swirling at times, and then coming to a standstill. Pavan let out a sigh. He turned around to look at them, his face pained.

"The answers aren't solid."

Brigit smirked and leaned to the right, her hand on her hip. Gesturing outward with her left hand, she dismissed the scrying. "I never liked those things. Ouija boards are more reliable. Why don't we query the ancestors for what we need? Hmm?" She was more comfortable and cockier now that she was in her Irish homeland near Belfast. "I'm sure they could give us more than enough information."

Rusalka huffed, sitting there atop a boulder in the middle of the grassy field they were in. Her legs were pulled up with her arms wrapped around her knees. Her head rested against them, cocked to the side, her long tresses cascading around her like a cloak. Even in childish petulance, she was still a beautiful creature. She reached out and plucked a reed from the grass, twirling it in her fingers.

Brigit sneered at her, annoyed at Rusalka's behavior, and turned her attention back to Pavan. "I mean it. Let's query the ancestors and get a solid answer."

"Fine. I'm out of options anyway, short of going in and simply taking our chances that it's the right time."

"Now is not the time to 'fly by the seat of our pants', Pavan."

"Of course, *priy*." Pavan bowed to Brigit and backed away, his linen clothing billowing behind him. If she wanted to query the ancient ones and her ancestors, she could be his guest. He loved his ancestors, but he didn't trust them. They hadn't always been the most reliable sources of information, in his experience.

Brigit clapped her hands, and a spark lit between them. She bent down to her pack, her red hair hiding her face for a moment, and pulled out a creased board. Unfolding it, she laid out her Ouija board in the dirt and pulled out a planchette. She'd had the courtesy of picking it up that time she had been in Spain for the Inquisition. It was taken off the hands of a gullible woman who had been dabbling in the occult. Said woman had paid the price for it, getting sent to the pyre, and Brigit was there to light the way, so to speak.

Placing the planchette on the board, Brigit delicately placed her first two fingertips of each hand on it and began to concentrate on her question. After a few minutes, the planchette began to move, slowly at first, then faster and faster, landing on a series of letters to spell out words and phrases in rapid-fire succession. After a time, it slowed down and stopped moving.

Brigit was enthralled, as she always was with the power of the board and her ancestors. Being in Ireland was empowering to her. Getting in tune with her ancestors was just icing on the proverbial cake. She looked up at Pavan and said one word.

Pavan nodded and glanced at Rusalka. Rusalka closed her eyes and sighed. The reed she had been twirling dropped from her hand and she sat upright. Stretching out her legs, she stood up and shook out her hair.

"Let's go."

The three of them collected their belongings and headed to the car. Each item went into the trunk, then they climbed into the vehicle with Pavan taking the wheel. Rusalka climbed into the back seat like the childlike figure she was. Brigit was too excited to care which seat she had and jumped into the passenger seat. The car engine roared to life, then settled into a purr like a kitten. Pavan steered them onto the dirt road and headed south.

They were on their way to destroy the vampires.

Chapter Six

Mo Shíorghra

The Garda were more than helpful.

Michael let Xander speak with them, explaining who they were and who Celie was. But they had to wait until the morning to get the release and authorization needed to seek out Celie. Once the Garda provided the location of the house she was staying at, they were off like a shot, headed there immediately. Luckily, the home was only a couple of miles up the road. Xander drove them there. Michael would have ported, but he feared anything that might spook Celie.

On arrival at *Teach Páirceanna Glasa*, they pulled into the driveway and parked in front of a brilliant barn. A black and white dog came running out, barking at them furiously in protective mode. A handful of ponies and some shaggy brown cows came over to a fence to stare at the intruders. Grunts and whinnies sounded across the laneway.

The day was ominous. The sky was heavy with blue-gray, low-lying clouds. A breeze blew from the east and rustled through the pasture, turning the grasses into a green ocean, rippling with each gust. Sunlight didn't dare break through the sky. Birds and insects were silent. The call of a lark came from across the fields.

Michael could feel something on the wind, something being carried toward them. It was dark and malevolent, powerful in intention. He didn't know what it was, but he knew what it meant for them. He knew what he needed to do, he just hoped he wasn't too late. Climbing out of the SUV that carried them, he closed his door and proceeded towards the house. Kat and Xander followed closely behind.

As he reached the front door of the house, it swung open. An old woman with white hair up in a bun, her body wrapped in a red shawl, stood there berating him in Irish. "Cé a cheapann tú atá tú? Ag teacht anseo, ag cur isteach ar an gcailín bocht seo!"

Without a thought, Michael was responding to her. "Mo leithscéal, a sheanmháthair." (My apologies, grandmother.) The woman froze; her bright blue eyes wide with surprise that he could speak the old tongue. However, Michael had been around a long, long time. "Ní iompar mé aon uacht drochintinn. Tá mé anseo chun mo ghrá a tarrthála." (I bear no ill will. I'm here to rescue my love.)

At these words, the woman's face softened into a smile, and she chuckled. "Why dinna ye say so? Come in! Come in!" She gestured to him, and after he walked in, she stopped when she saw Kat and Xander. "I dinna know ye, so I'll ask that you wait here." Then she shut the door on them.

Kat and Xander stood there in shock.

Inside, Michael took in his surroundings with a keen eye, noting several antiques and the simple creature comforts of the woman's home. The inside was warm and cozy, small and simplistic, with touches of handcrafted decor. He followed the woman from the front door through a parlor, wood planks creaking underfoot, and into a kitchen, where Celie was sitting at a tiny green table. On his entrance into the tiny room, she looked up at him and her breath caught. He smiled at her, and she seemed to soften ever so slightly at the gesture. Holding a cup of tea with both hands, she nodded to the seat across from her, so Michael walked over and sat down in the yellow wooden chair. It felt tiny, like a child's chair, beneath his large physique.

Fiadh took in the exchange and seemed satisfied. "Alright, Meri. I'll leave ye to it, t'en. But if ye need me, give a holler." She then exited out the room through a door leading to the pasture out back.

Michael turned his attention to Celie, who was eyeing him over her cup of tea. He cleared his throat before speaking. "I hope I wasn't intruding...?"

Celie shook her head no, her auburn hair swaying lightly. "No. Fiadh and I were just...chatting... about some people she used to know." She continued to eye him suspiciously, as if on guard and prepared for him to say or do something untoward. Michael grimaced inwardly at the notion he was still highly suspect to her.

"She seems like a very nice woman." His voice was quiet, as if he was concerned he might spook her.

Celie laughed, loud and fine, and this time it caught him off guard: he'd miss that sound so. "Fiadh would never dare to be called a 'nice woman'. She's a spunky troublemaker if ever there was one!" Celie laughed again at the thought of Fiadh as prim and proper. "She may be a grandmother, but she's a lively and feisty one."

Michael smiled, a full smile that reached his eyes, and he thought he saw himself reflected in Celie's. "I guess not. She gave me an earful when I arrived."

"That's my Fiadh." She was more relaxed now that she'd had a laugh, and he felt her warmth. His soul ached to touch her, hold her. Instead, he kept his hands flat on the table to convey his openness to her. He wanted everything about himself to reassure her.

After some silence, they each shared a moment of awkwardness. At the same time, they both began to speak.

"Now that I've found you–"

"After our meeting last night–"

"—I wanted to reintroduce myself to you."

"—we should really introduce ourselves."

They each stopped, then laughed heartily at the moment. It was a great way to begin.

Celie started things off first. "Oh. Yes, that probably would be a good idea, right? Let's begin with the obvious: What's your name?"

"Michael. Michael Hawkins."

"And I'm...?"

"Celie Moore. Er, well, Cecelia Moore, but everyone calls you Celie."

"Hmm...Celie... I'll give it that; it does sound more comfortable than Meri."

"Meri?"

Celie smiled a soft smile. "Fiadh's doing. She named me after America."

"Ah." A quiet chuckle escaped his soft, full lips. He watched Celie's gaze fall to his mouth, and it made him smile more.

"And where are you from, Michael?"

"The United States. A town called Bantum, but I was born and raised in the Boston area."

"Boston? That sounds familiar..." She stopped for a moment, then continued. "Am I from there? Boston, I mean..."

"Uh, no. You're with me in Bantum." Celie's eyes narrowed. "We live together."

At this, Celie blushed, her cheeks warming and coming alive with color. Her eyes sparkled and her nose crinkled just slightly. Michael felt stirrings in himself, and he fought against them. She was radiant when she bloomed.

"We do, huh?" Michael nodded. "And how long have we done that?"

Michael cleared his throat again. "About six months, give or take."

Celie looked down at her tea, pondering something for a minute. Then she looked back up at him, her green eyes shining like emeralds. "I must really like you."

Michael smiled again. Celie smiled in return, and it was like the sun lit up the world. "You could say that."

Celie laughed a little, self-conscious of herself and her barely concealed admission that she found him attractive. He could sense it, her desire for him. He was fighting against the natural urge to stand up, walk around the table, and kiss her senseless. It would be moot; she still didn't know him. Any extreme action on his part would just scare the hell out of her, and that was *not* what he or she needed right now. He needed to take this slow.

As slowly as he could anyway.

"Okay." She exhaled a deep breath. "So, I live with you – Michael Hawkins – in Bantum." Michael nodded. "What else should I know? Tell me more about you."

"Sure. I own an antique shop."

"Antiques?"

"Yes, and Xander works for me—er rather, with me."

"Xander?"

"The big guy that was with me last night."

"Oh okay. Hmm... Antiques... I can't say that suits you."

"Oh really?"

"You don't seem like an 'antiques' kind of guy."

Michael laughed. If only she knew...

"What about me?"

"Well, we already went over your name..."

"Right!"

"You used to work in insurance, but that's done. You didn't like it there anyway. You've been helping me out at the shop."

"Really? So we live together *and* work together?"

"That's right."

75

"Interesting..." Celie pondered this for a moment. All at once, she blurted out, "Where are my parents?"

This startled Michael, but just a little. "Your parents?"

"Yes. I've been wondering why they haven't come looking for me."

"Uh, your parents are... Well, they're not around anymore." Celie eyed him quizzically. "They've passed on."

Celie stiffened. "I see..."

"Not that it was recent. Well, not totally recent. Your mother died a couple of years ago. Your father passed last year, but you... The two of you were never close."

That was an understatement.

Celie internalized for a moment, seemingly lost in thought. Michael wanted to kick himself for his delivery, but it couldn't be helped. Telling someone their family was gone wasn't easy, no matter how it was said.

After a moment, Celie looked beyond her thoughts and back to him. "Well, that's that, then." She sighed heavily, then refocused her query. "Do I have any sisters or brothers?"

"No... However, you do have Kat, and she's as close as any sister could be."

"Kat?"

"Yes, she was also with me last night when we found you."

"Oh, with the light-colored hair?"

"Yes, that's right. She's outside, actually." He angled his head as if to gesture in her direction. "We all came today."

Celie glanced away from him down the corridor, toward the front door. After a moment, she turned her attention back to him and put down her teacup. "Best get this bandage ripped off already. Can you introduce me?"

Michael gave a nod and stood up. He held out his hand to help her stand up, something he had done his entire life. It was simply part of him to do things like that: holding a door open, pulling out a chair for a woman, et cetera. It was ingrained in him to behave chivalrously, and it was an inherent part of his character, especially at his age. Celie eyed his hand for a moment, then reached up to take it.

At the connection of their hands, Michael felt a searing heat, and he gripped her tightly. Celie startled and looked into his eyes. The storm there must have been alight, like lightning on the ocean. He stared back at her, willing her to see into his soul, to see the depths of his eternal love for her. She was his *mo shíorghra*, his soulmate, enduring in his heart and keeper of its flame. His soul *burned* for her. Nothing could stop the feelings that welled within him and shone in his eyes for her.

Celie stared at him, into his eyes, into their depths, for what seemed like an eternity. Did she remember? Could she? She had to have felt it at least, their connection reigniting. She had to; there were practically sparks flying. Michael swore he saw the embers. He watched her expectantly, but it must have been a trick of the mind. She eventually released his hand and looked away.

Sorrowfully, Michael regained his composure and followed her as she walked out of the room towards the front of the house.

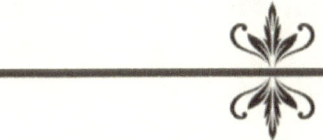

"And this is Xander." Kat gestured to the man standing next to her. Celie nodded a hello and turned her attention back to Kat.

"You two are together?"

"Oh yeah, baby." Xander nudged Kat, and she laughed. It was nice to hear her laughter, light and tinkling, and Celie smiled in response.

"How long have we known each other? The two of us?"

"Oh, a long time. A long, long time. Decades even."

"That does sound like a long time. But I'm not even sure..." she trailed off and then tilted her head to the side. "How old am I?"

Kat laughed. "Your birthday is November 17, 1989. Mine is June 3rd, but we've known each other since the eighth grade."

"So decades..." replied Celie and laughed. Kat laughed, too, and it was like something had righted within the world. Xander smiled at Kat and seemed to relax a little.

Kat continued spouting details to Celie: her favorite animal, her favorite color, her childhood celebrity crush, etc. She was following the instructions Michael had given them to a tee. She reminded Celie of her worst class in high school and her childhood bully. She even brought up that atrocious time they had gone clubbing in their early twenties. One of them had been stupid enough to drive home after a couple drinks. If there was anything Kat could remember, she told Celie using the tiniest details as if she was ticking each one off a checklist.

Michael watched the exchange continue and couldn't help but feel a pang of jealousy. Why was it so easy for Celie to connect with Kat? He wanted to regain his connection with her so badly it ate at him. He felt desperate. He knew how good their love was together, and he struggled under the weight of that knowledge. He also knew how much her friendship with Kat meant to her, but there was more at stake than a lifelong friendship.

Celie needed to remember who she was, *what she was*, and soon, before she turned feral.

It was at that moment that the wind blew softly, and again, Michael felt something coming towards them. He turned to the north and picked up smoke and spices on the wind. Whatever it was, whoever it was, it was getting nearer to them. He turned his attention back to Celie.

Michael interrupted their conversation. "Can we take a walk?" Celie's smiling face turned serious, and she nodded. Michael led Celie down the drive, Kat and Xander returning to the car to sit and talk.

As he walked, Michael unconsciously reached for Celie's hand. Whether she was aware of it or not, she took it, and Michael relished the feeling. Her skin was warm and soft, her hand held gently in his own. Michael felt his own skin tingling from the contact. Without thinking, he raised her hand to his lips and kissed her knuckles. He felt the warmth of Celie's blush without even having to look at her. Still, she didn't let go.

She didn't let go.

They walked in silence for a minute or two before Michael began to speak. "Do you remember anything?"

Celie took a deep breath, let it out slowly, then said, "No."

Michael sighed. "I know I'm just a stranger to you, but I want you to know that you can trust me."

Celie glanced at him. "Can I?"

"You can." He glanced at her, walking beside him. "I would never do anything to hurt you."

A few more steps passed by before she spoke. "How can I be sure?"

"I can only give you my word. And the word of Kat and Xander. I would say to trust your feelings, but I'm sure you're hesitant to give them too much sway."

"You're right about that. I'm not sure if my gut is being honest with me."

Michael turned toward her. "Celie..." She stopped and looked at him, and he felt his heart breaking with longing for her to see him, truly see him, the way she used to. "I promise you that I am the one person in your life who will always, now and forever, be faithfully true to you. No matter what."

Celie stared at him, then softly smiled. "Why do I believe you?"

"I just have one of those faces."

Celie laughed, and her laughter, her light, was a fire. It lit up the depths of his soul, and he welcomed the burn. He wanted to be all consumed by it.

"There's more you need to know, but I'm aware this has all probably been a lot for you."

"You've got that right." There was that sarcasm he missed. "I'm still trying to get used to my name, let alone all of you."

"That's fair, and I understand."

"Maybe you could come back tomorrow? We could talk more?" He could hear the hesitancy in her voice, and it made him want to wrap her in his arms and assure her everything was alright.

Michael smiled and felt her relax. "Of course."

They turned around and headed back to the house. Kat and Xander were already in the car, engine on. Michael stopped just behind the SUV and took Celie's other hand in his, holding both of them in his own.

"Continue to rest. We'll come back to see you tomorrow."

"Thank you," she whispered. Michael leaned forward, quietly inhaling the sunshine and sweet grass fragrance that lingered on her skin and placed a kiss on her cheek. When he pulled back, she was blushing again.

With that, he released her hands and headed to the car. As he pulled out of the driveway, he gazed in the rearview mirror, watching her as she stood in front of the house. She watched the car leave, clasping her hands in front of herself. She looked so small and alone, and it nearly broke him. He hated to leave her there, but until she remembered who she was, she was safer there than with him.

Once she was out of sight, he glanced at Kat and Xander in the backseat. They were staring at him quietly, expectantly. He knew what they were waiting for.

"Tomorrow, we'll tell her."

Something was coming.

Chapter Seven

Impressions

I woke from dreams I could barely remember. There were voices drifting to me on the wind, walls of water hovering to crash over me, flames as high as a Viking funeral pyre, and a man coming to me, telling me to not be afraid of him. Beyond that, it was quickly a distant memory as the light of the morning broke through my window.

I sat up and rubbed my eyes, yawning and stretching, then shrieking in pain as a headache blindsided me. I placed a palm over each eye and urged healing warmth into my head. I hoped the darkness would dissipate the stabbing sensations assaulting me, and eventually they did. As before, the pain disappeared and was replaced with a need to eat. I exhaled, having held my breath for a few seconds, and then swung my legs out of bed to stand up.

I dressed and went downstairs, greeting Fiadh in the kitchen. "Maidin mhaith, Fiadh."

"Meri! Maidin mhaith, cailín. How did ye sleep?" She sat at the table, a warm cup of tea in front of her, steaming in the morning light.

"Like the dead. Although I had some weird dreams?"

"Care to tell us about them?"

"No, I won't bother you with those. But I wanted to finish our conversation about what I saw the other day...?"

"Oh, Connor. My love. I miss him so..."

"So please tell me why I shouldn't go screaming into the hills because he was here?"

"I don't know, cailín. As I said yesterday, yer guess is as good as mine."

"I just wish I knew what was going on. Headaches, freakin' ghosts...what's next?"

"Still having the pains?"

"Yes, ma'am."

"All right t'en. We'll make sure we call the dochtúir again. Bleedin' devils never get t'eir fill."

"No, let's leave it alone for now. Right now I just need to eat." I went over to the icebox and began rummaging. "Do you have any more roast? Or a steak?"

"Sure t'ing. Check the back o'the box." Fiadh was watching me, suspicious at my behavior. I could feel her eyes boring into the back of my skull. I quickly grabbed the steak I found and took it to the stove to cook.

After barely a minute each side, I sat down at the table, my steak on a plate, and practically ripped it to shreds. Fiadh could barely contain her shock at my behavior, but the steak was just so incredibly delicious. A compulsion forced me to devour every bite, leaving no trace of the steak behind. Without compunction, I licked the plate clean. Fiadh's eyes were wide as saucers when I was done.

"Have a hankering for meat, do ye?" Disbelief was still etched across her face.

"You know, I really do?" I leaned back in my chair, sighing in satisfaction. "I'm not sure what's come over me, but that was scrumptious."

"Curiouser and curiouser..." Fiadh had an eyebrow raised in consternation.

I cleaned up my dishes and headed outside. I went about caring for Seamus, Willful, and the other animals on the farm when Michael's SUV pulled up, gravel crunching under the tires. This time, it was just him. No Kat or Xander to accompany him. He pulled into a spot alongside the fence where the ponies were lazing about.

As he climbed out of the vehicle, he looked around and spied me. His face lit up, and he grinned. It was a seriously happy grin, and I couldn't help but smile at him in return. I didn't know him well, but he seemed concerned for my well-being, and being around him was almost relaxing. It certainly didn't hurt that he was attractive and well-spoken. Dressed in black jeans, he had on a long black wool coat with a grey t-shirt underneath, and rugged black boots on his feet. He shut the car door and began to walk over to me, and I couldn't help but notice how much I loved his long, strong legs and his athletic gait.

I hoped that our conversation today would shed a little more light on things. I smiled at him as he approached. "Maidin mhaith, Michael."

Startled at my use of the vernacular, he smiled. "Well, well. Maidin mhaith, Celie. When did you start using the local tongue?"

"Oh, Fiadh's been teaching me. It's not hard to learn, or want to learn, around her."

"I bet. She's a special woman."

"Absolutely. She's told me stories about *Teach Pairceanna Glasa* and her life in Ireland. I feel like she's always got another story under her belt."

"Speaking of stories... We should talk more about you and me. Do you have time or are you in the middle of things?"

"No, no—I have time. Let me just finish putting this wheelbarrow away. I need to feed Seamus, too."

"Let me. I'm great with dogs." He immediately turned around to locate the pup. I saw Seamus hiding away around a hay bale. I called out to him, and he came forward, slightly skittish, but interested in meeting our visitor.

Before I could say or do anything, Michael had bent down and was scratching Seamus with fervor. Seamus had rolled over and was eagerly giving him access to his chest and belly. His tongue was hanging out the side of his mouth, and on his black and white face was the smile of a happy pooch. Clearly someone had made a best friend that day.

Once all the chores were taken care of, Michael escorted me to the house. My eyes were getting irritated by the bright light of the sunny day, and we thought it best to continue our talk inside. I offered him a drink, and after securing a bottle of stout beer for him from the kitchen, I met him in the parlor. He'd removed his coat and draped it over the sofa arm, leaving his short-sleeved T-shirt to bear witness to his muscular build.

A serious expression lingered on Michael's face. "How long has the sun been bothering you?"

Caught off guard, I handed him his beer. "Um, a couple of days, maybe? Why do you ask?"

"Have you been having any headaches?"

I paused. "Yeah. Just had one this morning. Why? What's this about?"

Michael sighed. "We don't have much time."

"Time for what?"

"I can help. But it's more than that. I can help you remember *you*."

"How?"

"You'll need to trust me."

"Uh...trust you to do what, exactly?"

Michael was silent for a moment, pensive even. "I'm going to delve into your memories and try to unlock them."

"Oh, is that all…" I rolled my eyes at the thought that he could do something like that. When my eyes were done rolling, they landed on his somber expression. Apparently, he meant what he said, or at least thought he did. I raised an eyebrow at him. "Wait—you're serious, aren't you?"

"Yes."

"Oh c'mon." I snorted. Yet, his face didn't change. "This is crazy! Are you going to hypnotize me or something?"

"No." Michael shook his head, growing frustrated. He tilted back his beer and downed it thoroughly. "Listen. I know you don't believe me, but we don't have the time to wax poetic about my methods or why this is so important."

"We don't?" I threw my hand on my hip and kicked it out for emphasis. "Well, you better make time, mister. I'm not about to let you play around with my head."

"No one will be playing around with your head."

"Or my emotions. You think this hasn't been difficult for me?"

"I know. No one is playing with your emotions either."

"So tell me what's going on."

"Fine." He huffed and exhaled, setting the empty bottle down on the nearest chair. "Here. Here's the lowdown on the entire situation, okay?" He pointed at himself. "I'm a vampire." He pointed at me. "You're a vampire." He gestured outward. "SpellCasters are out there, and if we don't restore your memories so we can fight them—together—then we're both dead."

I gulped. Audibly. "I'm sorry—say what?" This time both of my eyebrows were up.

"You. Are. A. vampire. So am I. And there are people—SpellCasters—who are trying to kill us." He practically sneered when he said their name. "I can prove this to you, but you have to trust me to unlock your memories."

I stood there, gawking at him like he had sprouted antlers or a third eye in his forehead.

"Celie...please... Let me help you. *Help us.*"

"I'm a...a..."

"A vampire."

I narrowed my eyes on his. "Get out."

"What?"

"I can't believe you would come here, give me some kind of hope that I could figure out who I am—*that* you *would know who I am*—and instead you give me some bullshit story like this?" As he stared at me, I scoffed, "You must think I'm some kind of idiot."

As I walked to the door, I muttered, "Serves me right for thinking the hot guy might be okay."

Once I had my hand on the door handle, I turned around to tell him to get out when I was rocked with a headache like before. This time, Michael was there to catch me when I stumbled forward and nearly fell. I gripped his arms tightly, in response to the pain and in an effort to steady myself.

"What the fuck," I said through gritted teeth.

"This is why we have to unlock your memories. You don't have much time."

"I...can't....believe...this is happening..." Bolts of searing agony flayed me open.

Michael held me close, saying nothing.

I didn't know what to believe. I had the electric boogaloo of pain dancing around in my noggin, the likes of which I hadn't dared to imagine possible. It was becoming more frequent, and that scared me. I had two options: I could believe Michael, or I could ignore him. What was the harm in indulging him with this bit of fantasy? What if it helped?

"You really think you're a vampire, huh?"

"I do—*I am*—and so are you."

I squeezed my eyes shut. "If I let you do this...will it hurt?"

"I promise it won't hurt."

"What happens... What if you can't do it? What if you can't fix this—fix me?"

"I won't let it come to that." He stroked my hair from my face as he held me close.

After a moment, the pain subsided, and I was simply holding onto *the* most stunning man who was gently smoothing my hair. Awkward as it was, I didn't want it to end. The smell of warm spices and sandalwood surrounded me like a comforting blanket. I could feel his muscles through his gray shirt, how they bunched and elongated as he helped me to stand up. He kept me close, and I distinctly felt him rest a hand on the back of my head, holding me still. I couldn't resist the urge to stay there, just for an extra moment.

"Okay." I felt him breathe, exhaling, and realized that he had been holding his breath. "Let's try this thing out. You. Me. The mind-meld, or whatever it is."

Michael pulled back, and I looked up at him. "You don't remember me but you know what a 'mind-meld' is?"

"They have Star Trek reruns here."

He grinned, and I felt myself falling into ridiculous feelings. Feelings that were sweet, feelings that were lustful, and feelings that were so welcoming that I couldn't fathom how I'd ever been away from them. I couldn't believe how quickly I was *feeling* for this man. True, real feelings—hence, they had to be ridiculous. Nothing this overwhelming could be anything less than absurd to the normal, average person. Yet here I was, with him, and feeling all of these messy things.

Just ridiculous.

"Perfect." He took my hand and led me over to the parlor sofa. I sat down, and he sat down next to me, our knees touching.

Truth be told, I wanted a lot more than that to be touching.

"Keep your body relaxed and keep your mind still. Think of a white room or a white wall. You want your thoughts to be as blank and empty as possible. Good. Now close your eyes. I'm going to hold your hand while we go through this, so I can maintain a physical connection to you."

"Okay." My eyes closed; I did my best to loosen up.

I began by willing my feet to relax, then my knees, then my hips, and so on up the chain to my head. I let myself sink into relaxation like it was a welcoming well of comfort. I pictured a blank white wall, no windows or anything, just simple, eggshell cream-colored. I focused on my breathing—in and out, in and out—and waited. And waited. And waited some more. I waited for what seemed like an eternity, but nothing happened.

I opened my eyes, and Michael sat there before me, his eyes closed, breathing gently. I stared at him for a few minutes before he opened one of his eyes. Steel gray stared out at me from under a chestnut brow. When he saw me watching him, he opened his other eye and looked at me expectantly.

"Anything?"

"No. I'm sorry."

"I was afraid of that. I encountered a lot of blockages, as if your memories had been encased in layers upon layers of steel. I was able to break through some, but I couldn't get through completely." He glowered. "They enacted something really nasty. Something immovable."

"So, what does it mean?"

"It means that we're going to have to go on a little adventure tonight."

"Oh really? And what do you mean by 'adventure'?"

Michael winked. "You'll find out."

We stared at each other for a minute or two, just looking into each other's eyes and being present. I could see the trust and hope inside Michael's. It was obvious he believed everything he was saying to me.

I couldn't lie to him. "You know... I don't believe. About the vampire thing."

"I know." He didn't seem bothered by it.

After a moment, a new question popped into my mind. "Can you tell me how we met?"

He smiled and proceeded to tell me how he had seen me around town in Bantum, and how I caught his eye. "It was your light," he said warmly, smiling just for me. From there, the story grew more complicated. He regaled me with tales of manifested dreams, a sinister cult, potential kidnapping, and my demonic father. He told me how he had decided to kidnap me before the cult did.

"The decision was easy: either you hate me, or you get stolen away by the bad guys."

"So, you thought abducting me was the way to go? With all the other possible options out there? *Abduction*?"

"Well, I was actually going to *ask* you to come with me...but you fainted at the sight of me, so... I didn't have much choice at that point."

"I fainted? Really?" I snorted, then blushed in embarrassment.

Michael just laughed and pointed a finger at me. "There—that's the Celie I know."

My breath caught in my throat. Michael really believed he knew me through and through. I was both interested in learning more but also frightened of what else I might find out. "What happened when I woke up?"

"You tried to escape but things were locked down. Mostly you were just frustrated because you recognized me and trusted me but had no idea why. The whole situation really went against the grain for you. You're not really a 'damsel in distress' kind of girl."

"Damn right. I hate girls who wait for a rescue. I mean, figure it out your damn self, right?"

He smirked. "Well, I rescued you anyway, and I told you all about me and what was going on. I came clean to you about the dreams, and who I am. *What* I am. You took it surprisingly well, actually." He smiled at the memory.

"Can you tell me just how you convinced me about any of this?"

"Really?"

"Yeah."

"Well, I... Uh..."

"Seriously. If you were able to convince me of being a vampire before, you should be able to do it again."

"Okay. If you're sure..."

"Absolutely." I felt one hundred percent confident he was going to pull some Dracula-style maneuver on me and whip out a cape.

"Here goes."

Michael opened his mouth, and each of his two canines elongated into dagger-like fangs.

"Whoa..." I reached out and tapped one with my finger. He closed his mouth so fast; I barely got my finger out in time.

"Why do you *insist* on doing that?"

"Oh? I've done that before?"

"For the love of god, woman, you are on repeat."

I laughed. "At least I know I'm consistent." Michael laughed, too. The laughter felt good, felt healing, but then, just as quickly, we both sobered up.

"So..."

"So..."

"And I'm... I'm like you? I can do that with my teeth?"

"You can. But we'll talk more about that tonight. We're going to get your memory back if it kills me."

"Let's hope it doesn't come to that." I couldn't help but be curious. "What do you have in mind?"

"You'll see. For now, I want you to rest. I'll be back here to pick you up at eight o'clock," he said standing.

I stood to follow him, and I continued to hold one of his hands as he walked to the front door. When he reached it, he turned around and began to raise my hand up to his lips. However, he turned my palm over and placed a kiss on the inside of my wrist. The intimacy of the act was so startling I held my breath without thinking. I released it as he released his kiss, and my skin felt cold where his warm lips had just been.

"Until tonight," he whispered. Then Michael released my hand and headed to the SUV. I watched him climb in, shut the door, and start the engine. I didn't look away, in fact, until he had driven out of the driveway and down the road. A small dust cloud billowed up into the sky. I sighed.

I was beyond ridiculous for him.

Chapter Eight

Wild Girl

Nighttime came, and I anticipated devilry.

Michael showed up right on time to collect me. I met him outside, climbing into the SUV with him, and he took off out of the driveway. No one else was with us. The night air was cool, and I clenched my jacket tighter around myself. The SUV headlights shone through the dark, illuminating the dust that spilled upward from the dirt road as he drove on into the night.

I wasn't sure where we were headed, but Michael had promised me that it was going to help me remember. I sighed. I wasn't expecting much, but there was something about him, something that felt achingly familiar to me. I trusted him. Maybe I shouldn't? I couldn't say except that when he touched me, it was spontaneous combustion. I felt fire in his touch, and I knew that meant something. I just had to find out what.

I told him I had another headache while he was gone, and he winced. "It wasn't pleasant."

"I have no doubt. Is there anything else that you've noticed with these headaches? Anything you feel is unusual?" He focused on the road, avoiding looking at me.

"Now that you mention it, yes. I mean, I don't know if it's really unusual or not, but it is for me. I've been having these insatiable cravings for steak?" Michael glanced at me. "I know, right? Totally weird."

"Not at all."

"No?"

"No."

"Okay, well then, other than the bright light issue, that's it."

"That's enough," murmured Michael.

"What does it mean?" I asked.

"It means that we're almost out of time."

"Out of time for what?"

Michael refused to look at me. He focused on the road ahead, and I frowned. I hated not being told what was going on. I glanced at him, wondering what he knew but wasn't telling me. Because he was refusing to look at me, I decided to try something new. I reached out and took his hand. That definitely caused a ruckus. He jerked the wheel a little and shot a look of surprise my way. In defiance, I held on, and he seemed to relax ever so slightly. I took some initiative and stroked the back of his hand. He continued to relax behind the wheel, and I thought I saw a small smile creep across his face.

"Where are we headed?"

"I'm taking you somewhere that we can try to get your memory boosted."

"Where's that?"

"Mountbellew."

"Mountbellew?"

"Yes. It's just south of here."

"What's there?"

94

"A place that will help."

I sighed. Getting information out of him was like pulling teeth from a crocodile. "Okay." I hated having to wait for more info. I let him drive in silence.

After a few more miles, I couldn't contain myself anymore. "Are you *always* this much of a talker?" That got a deep rumble of a laugh out of him, and I couldn't help but smile. His laughter and smile made him even more handsome.

We drove on through the night, but surprisingly *not* in complete silence. The radio was turned on, and we listened to some local music and compared notes on our favorite songs they played. Oddly enough, we seemed to love the same songs that we heard. Michael even provided notes on some bands that we had mutually in common: Toto, Dance with the Dead, Gunship, Billy Joel, The Midnight, etc. Many I didn't remember, but some seemed to tickle the back of my brain. Apparently, I was very interested in music from the eighties and synthwave.

"Synthwave?"

"Yes," replied Michael. "It's like an homage to the synthesizers of the 1980s, but the music is all new. There's darksynth, retrowave, outrun: close to a dozen stylizations of it. A lot of movies and TV series have been using it for soundtracks lately, too. Most of them you love."

"Neat. I'll have to check it out—or remember it. Something like that," I said, laughing.

"Something like that," he repeated and smiled. I really loved his smile.

We continued to drive on through the night, talking about simple things, and commenting on things we saw during the drive. I could see ruins and stone cottages highlighted by the moonlight. It may have been dark out, but Ireland was filled with scenery. Plus, we were getting along so well, and I didn't want the conversation with Michael to end.

A short time later, we arrived in Mountbellew, an Irish town to the southwest of Roscommon. There were ancient stone structures and historic buildings, but very few people—just several hundred, in fact. It was a tiny hamlet off a main road, located in the lush greenery of Ireland.

Once in the town limits, Michael drove to a park that contained a 'walled garden'. There were stone walls reaching twelve to fifteen feet high, surrounded by green forests. We parked nearby and got out. As we walked to the wall opening, Michael took my hand in his, and I let him. I marveled at the ancient history here. Inside the garden were remnants of more stone structures. Ivy crawled high and vast along the walls. We walked inside.

A blinding headache struck me as we crossed the threshold. I fell to my knees, gravel stone cutting through my pants into my skin. Michael grabbed a hold of me and helped me up. He steadied me as we made our way to a bench inside the walls. I managed to sit down just in time before a heavy bout of nausea overcame me. I leaned forward and retched, completely embarrassed that this was happening in front of Michael. A headache was one thing, but vomit was something else.

"Sorry I destroyed...this beautiful...place..." I said between desperate attempts to catch my breath.

Michael sat next to me, rubbing my back. "It's okay. I'm sure the garden will survive."

"What are we doing here?" A minute later, I had gathered enough strength to sit up. The headache was fading into the background now, but again there was a strong need to eat. I felt like I was starving, and I couldn't seem to banish the idea of meat. Glorious meat.

It must have been the sickness.

"We're here so I can use the power of the garden. It's going to help me push through the blockade they built in your memory banks."

"There's power here?"

"There's power everywhere in Ireland. This is just one of many seats of magic, a place of wisdom and ancient vibrations. It seemed like the best place to bring you, so we can resolve this and get you back to normal."

"I wish I knew what normal was. I don't feel like I've been normal in a very long time."

"Fair enough."

We moved benches, for obvious reasons, then Michael asked me to go back into a meditative, trance-like state. I worked on myself like before, closing my eyes. I let myself sink into the sensation—or lack thereof—of relaxation, starting at my feet and working my way up. Then I pictured a blank white wall. It was a struggle, but the quiet of the garden was definitely helpful.

This time I felt Michael's breathing match my own. I felt him pushing at the boundaries of my mind, nudging the memories and seeping into my brain like water spreading sand. It didn't hurt, though. It actually felt...nice, like a heavy warmth settling over me, which was a great contrast to the cool night air.

We sat in silence as I let him work his 'magic' on me. I focused on the white wall, on his breathing, on being in the moment and letting myself sink away. Each moment felt like an eternity of comfort and calming tranquility.

Then I felt it, something bright opened in my mind, like a beam of light shining down on me but spilling out from my limbs and eyes. I opened my eyes but couldn't see anything; it was too bright. The light was everywhere and everything. Afraid of what this meant, I called out to him.

"Michael!"

"I'm here, Celie."

"What's going on? It's too bright—I... I can't see!"

"I'm almost there..." All of a sudden, I felt his grip on my hands tense.

It hit me hard: a sudden rush of air, a breeze pushing at me from behind, then swooping up and back down from above. My hair wrapped around my face, poking my eyes and tickling my nose. I closed my eyes again. The wind continued to wrap around me, swirling around me faster and faster, and my insides jumped and toppled over each other.

As soon as it had begun, it stopped, and everything grew calm. Eventually I felt the light leave, and there was a stillness permeating the air, so I opened my eyes. In the place of the light was something new, something familiar.

Everything I had been missing, all of my memories, came flooding back like water washing over me. Startled, I began sucking in air like I had been deprived of oxygen. I frantically grabbed at Michael, and he steadied me. Then slower still, I inhaled and took in the night air, breathing in everything that was me. My past, my life, my friends, my love: all of it was mine again. I exhaled slowly and opened my eyes. Michael was staring at me, anticipation in every feature.

I immediately reached out and hugged him, anxious to feel him against me and be in his arms. He held me close, and I felt him rest his chin on my head. We both sighed heavily with relief.

I was back.

"Thank you. I can never repay you for what you've done for me."

"You never have to." He kissed the top of my head. Then he pulled me away from him and looked me over. "You remember it all now?"

"Yes. Everything. Every moment. Every single bit."

"Thank god."

"I'm sorry for anything I put you through."

"No apologies are necessary, Celie. There was nothing you could have done to prevent this."

"I could have fought. We knew they were coming. I could have gotten through their damn spell."

"No. No, you couldn't. This was ancient magic. They cast something deep and powerful over both of us. We're just lucky that we have our own magic on our side."

"How did you break free? Are you just stronger than me?"

"No. No I'm not."

I looked at him expectantly. He was clearly holding something back.

He finally spoke up. "A demon came to my aid when I needed protection. They tried to kill me."

"Did you kill them?"

"Yes. I killed the one with earth magic. A demoness named Meyana."

"Good. I hope she burns."

Michael paused before speaking again. "She...she took advantage of me, of our situation."

"What do you mean 'took advantage'?"

"That spell, the one that cast us apart..."

"Right..." I didn't like where this was headed.

"It didn't just drop you off here, and it didn't just give *you* amnesia. It gave me amnesia as well."

"They wiped your memory?"

"Yes."

I thought on this for a minute, then realized what he was saying. "Oh my god, Mike. Oh my god, oh my god, oh my god..."

"If I had known–"

"Known what? That she was going to rape you, and you would be a willing participant? Holy fuck..." I was shouting as I began pacing back and forth. "That bitch! That evil, maniacal, fuckety-fuck, lousy *bitch*!"

Michael was silent, not looking at me, unable to bring himself to do it. I stopped in front of him and knelt down. "You know I don't blame you...right? It hurts, of course. Boy, does this sting something fierce, but I do *not* blame you."

"Kat sure does..."

"Kat can suck it. I don't blame you. Do you hear me? You didn't know."

Michael looked at me, tears in his eyes. A singular one fell down his cheek, and I gently wiped it away. He definitely believed this was his fault. "How can you not? I remember everything, Celie. *Everything*. I remember the words I said, what I felt, what I did—and I *hate* myself for it. It may have been a spell, but it was still me—*this body*—that did those things."

The sadness and anger in his voice were like a poisoned dagger to my heart. I stopped breathing for a minute, realizing that he was torturing himself with memories. Memories of his own making, yes, but not memories of his own volition.

"Look at me." I took his face and forced him to look me in the eyes. "You may have memories, but they aren't yours. Not really. Not truly. This is like a bad dream, and we're both just waking up from it." I paused. "We have each other now, right?" He nodded. "So that's all there is. Me and you. You and me."

"We still have three more."

At that moment, I remembered my visitor and the unknown compatriots in his vehicle. I felt my breath leave me. "They were here..."

Michael's brow furrowed. "What do you mean?"

"They were here. Here in Ireland. They came to see me!"

"What?!"

"Yes. I hadn't been here for long, but they found me along the road to Fiadh's house."

"Tell me everything they said."

"The tall man-"

"Wind."

"Yes. The one who controlled air. He approached me. There were two other people in the car with him, but I never saw their faces."

"Go on..."

"I thought he seemed familiar, so I asked if we knew each other. He seemed to find that funny, but I couldn't place him. I told him it must be a mistake and that I was sorry for asking. Then he left in his car."

"And that's it?"

"That's it."

"Okay, so they know where you are. I wonder why they didn't bother to kill you, especially with your amnesia. No memory, no me, new country, guard down; you were an easy target."

I flinched. "I'm no one's target, Mike."

Michael's face softened. "I'm sorry. I just meant that they had us separated, and if they wanted us both gone, why not just do it? Why prolong things with these games?"

I lowered my eyes. "It sure didn't feel like a game to me. I had no memory of anything. Nothing. Nothing was familiar." I glanced up at him again. "I can't believe that I lost you, that I lost us. How could I do that? How could I just forget us and everything we have? Everything we've been through?"

Michael smiled at me. "None of that matters. All that matters is that we've found each other again. Nothing can keep us apart. We're in this together for the long haul; we should both know that by now."

"We really should," I said, chuckling, then I stopped. "Oh my gosh: Fiadh! How am I going to explain this to her? And how can I leave her? I love that little old woman!"

"We'll visit her every few months, and set her up with a video platform, so we can talk with her regularly. I won't let you go through life never seeing her again."

"Good. Better yet, don't ever let me go anywhere. I never want to be away from you again."

"Oh, you can count on that." I loved the way he embraced me.

We held each other, just like that, for what felt like forever. Nothing else mattered. We had finally come back together, reunited after all this time. I couldn't believe I had my memories back, no longer living in ignorance of my life. I looked up at him and touched the side of his face, memorizing again the angles of his cheekbones and the line of his jaw. He leaned in and kissed my eyelids, and I shivered. We gazed into each other's eyes and just breathed, and it was like our lives were complete again.

Without any warning, my vision began to blur, darkness creeping it at the edges. I blinked furiously in an attempt to get it to go away, but it remained. My stomach began to turn over again, but instead of heaving, my internal organs seemed to be gripped by some unseen force. It felt like they were being squeezed, harder and tighter, until I felt like I couldn't breathe. I doubled over.

"Celie? What is it?"

"Something's—something's wrong." I gasped and struggled to vocalize what I was feeling, the internal sensations causing me to turn away from him.

"What's happening?" His concern was palpable.

"I...I don't know..." I coughed. There was blood.

Next to me, I felt Michael stiffen at the sight. "Oh my god."

"What is it?" Cough. Cough. "What—ow!—what is going on? My insides—they feel like they're being squeezed in a vise!"

"You're turning." He abruptly vanished, disappearing into nothing. He straight up 'poofed' out on me.

I spun around, stunned that Michael would leave me so quickly now that we had been reunited. Yet, after a moment, he appeared right back in front of me. He had a pouch in his hand. It was my favorite: A-positive blood, so sweet and fresh.

Before he could rip it open for me, I slapped him, then I grabbed the sides of my own head. "What's happening to me...?" I cried as my vision clarified and turned red. Blood red. I looked up at Michael and he looked concerned, and afraid...and somehow so far away. My insides clenched tighter within me...

...And the pain was a wrecking ball...

...The pain was...

...The pain...

Suddenly I wasn't myself anymore; I was gone. There was no Celie, no ex-insurance worker, no lover of synthwave. There was no American girl, no woman with memory loss, no newcomer to Roscommon. There was no best friend of Kat or houseguest of Fiadh Murphy. There was no lost love of Michael's life. There was no *me*.

I was simply hungry.

Famished.

Ravenous.

I swung around and growled at the tall creature in my way, shoving it aside like it was a paper doll. It went airborne and landed across the pond, nearly 40 feet away. I ran towards the nearest opening in the wall, grasping at the stones and looking around for predators. Then I ran across the gravel road and into the woods. Branches scratched at my body, tangled in my hair, swiped at my face. The scent of my own blood filled my nostrils and made me ache. Yet none of it mattered. I kept running, desperate for something to satisfy the hunger I felt, the urge, the craving.

I needed to feed.

Michael watched Celie disappear into the woods, her snarls disappearing into the night air. Breathing hard, his bones repairing quickly from the impact, he sat up from the ground and pulled out his cell phone. He felt fortunate that it still worked, despite the cracked screen. He dialed Xander immediately.

"We're in trouble."

"It didn't work?"

"Oh, it worked, but she's gone feral."

"Oh shit."

"'Oh shit' is right."

Ionsáiteán

Avenge

"*Mujhe bachao.*" 'Save me'.

Pavan was overwhelmed being in the car with Brigit and Rusalka. They were like two halves of the same coin, and he couldn't bear it. Where one was harsh, one was soft. Where one was smart, one was dense. Spending all this time with them was like a punishment, and he desperately wanted out.

"*Merzkoye sushchestvo!*" Rusalka had taken to shouting from the backseat. She was petulant, tired of the insults landed on her by Brigit, and was now calling her names in Russian.

Brigit flipped around in the front seat to glare at her. "Oy, what did you call me? I'll have your neck when I find out!" She was too busy trying to get Pavan to drive the right way that she couldn't be bothered with Rusalka's pity party. She turned back around to focus on the map in her hands. "No, we need to take N-54."

"I know that."

"So why aren't you taking it?"

"Leave me be, woman."

"Woman? Don't you dare take that tone with me, Pavan."

"Sorry, Brigit." He muttered "*daanav*" under his breath. "I'm taking N-54 now."

They were not far from where they would meet up with the vampires and dispatch them. Pavan knew they would not play with them as they had done before. This time they would be carefully destroyed as originally intended.

It wasn't his idea to spellcast them the way they had, having indulged Brigit in one of her typical fantasies. She was very...*apamaanajanak*, abusive and twisted in her way of thinking. She often wanted to do things that meant taking risks they couldn't otherwise afford. In this case, it meant separating the lovers and toying with them: mentally, emotionally, and physically.

It wasn't what he would have chosen to do, and he was frustrated.

If only Meyana was here...

She had been their best leader of the past two-hundred years. However, they had each felt her passing when it struck those few days past. One moment her warmth could be felt across the oceans, and then suddenly she was no more. An emptiness in their collective group. Having spent so much time together, the lack of her presence was significant. They knew that the vampire she had been left in charge of had succeeded in killing her. They vowed that when the time was right, they would attack him and the amnesiac one here in Ireland, getting rid of both of them in one fell stroke.

Pavan kept driving, his window down, the road winds softly tousling his hair. He inhaled deeply and let his breath out slowly. The air rejuvenated him, and he let it soften his demeanor, so he could continue dealing with the two Casters in the car. He focused on the drive, the sensation of the road under the tires, the feeling of the leather steering wheel beneath his fingers as he gripped it harder.

He would ignore the childish banter in the car.

He would avenge Meyana.

Chapter Nine

Raw

Michael Hawkins had lived through centuries of time and all over the world. He had been present for the dismantling of the Berlin wall, he had seen the first radio device debut to civilization, and he had helped the Native Americans fight back against soldiers seeking to displace them from their lands. He had even assisted Benjamin Franklin in his kite test with electricity. All of this and more, he had witnessed.

Today, Michael was witness to the transformation of his soulmate into a feral being, one capable of ravaging unimaginable horrors on innocent human flesh.

Michael was back at the hotel, having informed Xander and Kat of their newest problem. Before heading out after Celie, he needed to feed, and the pouch he had brought for her was destroyed in the incident. He explained what happened in Mountbellew. Neither of them took it well.

"How *could* you! Of all the selfish, egotistical things you could've done..." She lunged at Michael, claws out to enact revenge, but Xander stopped her. He grabbed her by her arms and held her back, using more strength than he would have liked to admit. "At any given time, you could've slipped her some of that damn A-positive shit and stopped this in its tracks! But no. No, you seemed to think you had it all under control—"

"I did. At least, I thought I did..."

"Oh really? This shitshow is your idea of 'under control'?" She whipped her head to the side, looking back at Xander, who still held her in place. "You better let me go, or so help me..."

Xander frowned. "I can't do that, Kat."

"I'll kill you." She turned her head back toward Michael. "I'll kill you both."

"You're out of control, and that's not going to help Celie," said Xander.

"Oh, like this guy helped her?!" Incredulous, she began to cry out of frustration and anger, sadness and outrage warring within her svelte frame. "She's all alone, and now she doesn't even know she's human!"

"Vampire..."

"I can't believe she's gone again!" She struggled to free herself, but after a few minutes of crying, she was spent.

Xander slowly eased up his hold on Kat, whose head was now hanging down, her chin touching her chest. He could feel the exhaustion creeping in and her energy dwindling. He gently released her arms, easing her down, and she crumpled into a heap at his feet. He looked up at Michael, pissed.

"You really fucked this up, Mike. Royally fucked this up."

"I know." Michael stood staring out the window of the hotel room, drinking from the blood pouch. He couldn't bring himself to look at Xander.

"I'm not going to say much; just know that I don't disagree with Kat's take on things. But that's not gonna help anyone right now. Right now, we have to keep our wits about us and go find your girl."

"If we can find her..."

"Oh, fuck that noise. Stop being a little bitch and get your head out of your ass." At Xander's harsh words, Michael raised an eyebrow and turned to look at Xander. "We have to canvas for her, search the countryside. Ireland is exactly that: a fucking island. There's only so far she can go. We'll find her. But right now, I need you to stop acting like your dog died and get your head in the game."

The impromptu lecture actually did help Michael 'get his head out of his ass'. He realized he was wallowing, wading into self-pity at the situation instead of doing something about it. First, he threw out the drained pouch, then he gritted his teeth and straightened himself out, pulling on his t-shirt to get it right. He turned around and nodded to Xander, saying nothing. He knew actions would speak louder than words right now. Striding to the hotel door, Michael walked out, leaving Xander with Kat, and closed the door behind himself.

Outside, gray clouds hung low, a light mist filling the air and clinging to each passerby. The air was cool, so Michael went to the SUV and grabbed out a hooded sweatshirt. Pulling it on, he looked around and watched as a man walked into the hotel lobby. Once no one else was around, Michael vanished.

Xander watched from inside the hotel room as Michael disappeared. Turning away from the window, he walked over to where Kat was on the floor. He gently picked her up and sat her on the bed. She took the opportunity to lay on her right side and curl up into the fetal position. Xander laid down and curled up against her back, spooning her and wrapping his arms around her. He heard her take a shaky breath.

"It'll be alright." His breath was warm against her left ear.

It took a few minutes, but eventually Kat spoke up. "How? How does she come back from this?"

Xander had no answer. He'd thought about it, too. Celie had never killed a person before—at least, not an innocent. With all of his time with the military and the government, he knew what it meant to have to take a life. But even he had been blessed with not knowing the repercussions of collateral damage. He'd been lucky enough to avoid that on his own record.

Who knew how this would change her? Who knew what this would do to her? What impact would this have on the Celie they knew and cared for?

There, with the hotel curtains drawn, Xander held onto Kat, and they simply breathed together.

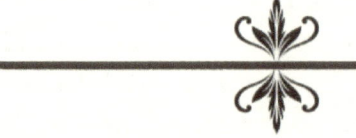

Reappearing in Mountbellew, Michael began tracking Celie's movements. He started at the walled garden and headed across the dirt road into the woods. Following her trail was difficult, but for all the wrong reasons. He could see her movements as if she was there, moving just ahead of him, the ghost of her running erratically through the trees. Yet it was the idea that she had lost all semblance of humanity that drove him through the forest, desperately and eagerly.

Celie was a wild thing now. A child of the most basic needs: food, shelter, breath. She had no need for him or any of her friends. No need to smile, laugh, sleep, or eat. She only needed to drink, to feed, to find the next victim to slate her bloodlust.

This was what drove Michael forward. At each break in a tree limb, at each track in the dirt, he pushed onward, knowing each one would lead him closer to Celie. And he couldn't let her go. Not this time, not any time. She was the other half of his soul, the part of him he'd thought he lost all those years ago. Each step forward was one that would get Michael nearer to her.

Xander and Kat were right, thought Michael as he ran through the trees. He had failed to protect Celie from the dangers of the vampire world. He'd never thought it would have come to this, and that was the key to his failings: his arrogance and his ignorance. He'd thought he had more time. Michael had believed he could 'beat the system' at its own game, putting his relationship with her above her own welfare. Despite knowing it was all going down, he didn't act as he should have.

Yet again, Michael was struggling to make things right.

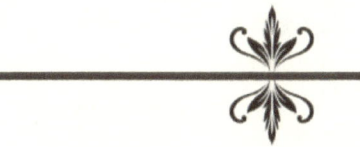

I felt nothing but maddening hunger, an ache within that had shattered my sanity in two and drove me across the Irish countryside. I was seeking satiety, seeking fulfillment, seeking something I could no longer define with mere words. The hunger was driving me towards people, the source of my would-be satisfaction, and I pushed through the woods until I encountered them.

It was a small house, long and white with black shutters. The white exterior walls were dingy, with ivy growing here and there, up and over the edges of the gray roof. A small, black compact car sat in the driveway in front of a detached garage. The house was quiet from the outside, but even from across the field, I could see movement inside one of the windows that dotted the house walls.

Afterall, my senses had grown keener with the lack of a conscience.

My stomach grumbled as I moved quickly to the house, sniffing the air and checking my surroundings. No other movement across the fields: no cars, no people, no animals. The only thing I saw was a hawk circling overhead, and I snarled at it. I could smell the blood inside the house, and nothing would stop me from getting to it. As I reached the backdoor, I found it unlocked. The doorknob turned easily, and I slunk inside, leaving it open behind me.

I had only one thing on my mind...

Michael came to a golden field swaying in the cool breeze and stopped. It was barren except for a house on the far end. A lazy hawk circled in the sky above, and he watched it for a moment, envious of its simplicity in nature. He went back to surveying the field when he heard it: a shriek, someone crying out in horror. He knew it came from the house, and he vanished, reappearing less than 20 feet from the structure.

The house was not quiet. Michael pushed beyond the backdoor and into the house, anxious to find the person who was wailing. He wanted to save the source of the screams, but more urgently, he wanted to save the cause of them.

I was in the middle of things when another creature appeared in the room, emerging out of nowhere. My food was screaming in my ear, but I didn't let it go. I couldn't let it go. All I wanted was to keep feeding. All I *needed* was to keep feeding. The sweet smell of blood filled my nostrils, and I inhaled deeply. Yet my instincts told me the creature was my enemy. I threw my food down on the ground, and it tried to crawl away from me. I snarled and grabbed its leg, pulling it close and insisting it stay nearby. Then I turned my attention to the creature.

Michael saw Celie in her raw form and flinched. Her eyes were redder than her disheveled hair, her clothing in shambles. Her teeth were elongated and dripping with blood, the viscous liquid smeared across her cheeks, chin and chest. He could hear the fluid in her lungs as she breathed. Her ears had grown larger, pointed and dark like a bat's, and her nails were grown out into dagger-like claws. She was growling at him, watching intently, clearly considering him an enemy. Her legs were in a wide stance, braced for whatever was going to come next. Her left hand was latched onto the leg of a woman who was desperate to get away from the punishment.

Michael knew what he had to do.

I was prepared to defend myself against this thing that had invaded my space and stopped my meal. My precious meal. I was still starving, desperate for more. The taste, the texture, the hunger... But this creature, this thing had come barging in and wanted to take it from me. I could *feel* it. I couldn't let myself blink, couldn't do anything but breathe and lick my lips for more of the delicious taste.

That was how I saw it disappear.

I snarled in surprise, looking to my left and my right. Before I could turn around, it had me in its grasp, holding me in place at my sides. I howled. Having abandoned the hold on my food, I kicked and clawed at the creature, hearing it groan as I scratched and fought. I flung my head back and landed a blow. Despite my own pain, I was energized as it released me and fell forward, scrambling away. I quickly turned around to face it. The creature was staring at me, then disappeared again.

I froze, then retreated against a wall. Suddenly it was back and in my face. It grabbed my arms and snarled at me, teeth long and sharp coming within inches of my face, and I froze again. What was this? Something about it seemed familiar. I growled back at it and tried to bite it; I missed. I kept trying. It simply stood there, holding me in place as I writhed and struggled, bit and kicked.

Eventually I grew tired and went slack. As soon as I felt it lighten the tension on my limbs, I fought again, using all of my strength. My breath came in heaves as I struggled to simply be free. The creature merely growled at me and tightened its grip.

Minutes of struggle turned into hours. After what seemed like forever, I finally caved. My strength was gone. I was still ravenous, but I could no longer fight. I crumbled in the creature's arms, still breathing heavily and snapping. I looked around for my food but it was gone. I whined, then snarled in aggravation.

Michael continued to hold Celie powerfully in place despite her collapse. He couldn't let her escape, and she was still giving signs of struggle. He heard her whine, and it nearly broke him. It was heartbreaking to see her like this. She had de-evolved into a primal, feral version of herself, and he was to blame. Her raw desperation for blood was overwhelming her, and it wrenched at him. He felt tears well up in his eyes and a painful ache crawl up from his chest, but he swallowed it down. He had to be strong for her, for both of them.

Celie slid downward as he released her arms, slumping to the floor. Her defeat was real. She continued to alternate between whines and snarls as she lay there, and Michael knelt down beside her. She looked at him, growling and grimacing with pain as the hunger wracked her frame. Michael tried to reach out to her, to touch her cheek, but she flinched away from him, so he pulled back. She was devastatingly spent by the changes she had undergone.

Grabbing some nearby curtain ropes, Michael took Celie's hands and put them behind her back, tying them together to keep her from hurting others or himself. Then he picked her up, guttural sounds emanating from her throat as she made small writhing movements, twisting at her bonds. He put her over his shoulder and then ported them back to the alley behind the hotel. Once there, he put her down and led her to the room. It was difficult, as she struggled to walk, and he struggled not to be indisputably obvious with her snarling form. When he reached the hotel room door, he knocked first before entering. Then he opened the door and pulled Celie inside, closing the door behind her.

"Oh...my...god..." Kat was standing by the bed, staring at Celie with her jaw agape. Her chin length hair was a little messy, and she was in sweatpants now.

Michael winced at her voice. "I found her." He avoided Kat's eyes, hoping to steer clear of any more blame game rhetoric. He was focused on getting Celie well and prayed that Kat would be, too.

Xander came out of the bathroom, a beige towel around his waist, and Michael heard him gasp. Clearly neither of them had expected this to be the full state of Celie having gone feral. On that note, he was responsible there, too. He never prepared them for what her raw form would look like. He winced again.

Michael led Celie to a chair in the corner and sat her down. She growled at him, and he swore that she hissed a little. Out of sheer instinct, he hissed back, and she quieted, her grimace turning into a quizzical look.

He turned to Kat and Xander, who had joined Kat near the bed. Xander held a towel in his hand and had it twisted up tightly. Kat was grabbing onto Xander's arm. They were both staring at Celie as if they had seen a ghost.

"Here she is. Take a good look. This is what happens when we don't feed regularly."

"Good god..." Xander gulped audibly.

For a while, all Michael could hear was Celie's breathing. "Now that that's over with, here's what I need from you to help me fix her: we have to watch her, we have to feed her, and we have to keep her here. We can't let anyone in this room, no matter what. If she gets out, that's on *all of us*. Do you understand?"

Xander and Kat nodded their heads in agreement.

"Once we have her fed, we have to watch her to see how she responds. It's going to take a day or two before we see the effects start to take hold." Michael closed his eyes and took a deep breath. "When Celie—that is, the Celie *we know*—starts to come around, we're going to have to be there for her as she realizes what she's done."

He heard a slight, breathy inhale, then Kat spoke up. "And what was it...that she's done...?"

"She killed a woman."

Kat began to cry, soft tears of heartbreak, and Xander muttered some curse words under his breath. Michael opened his eyes and looked down at his love, as she growled and gnashed at him. She was still writhing in her bindings, but she wasn't going anywhere. She was in this position because of him, and he would be damned if he wasn't going to get her out.

On that note, Michael headed towards the mini fridge in the room and opened it. He reached inside and pulled out a pouch of O-negative blood, best used in universal donor-type situations. He figured this was an ideal situation to give her something appealing to all discerning vampire blood lusts. He ripped the pouch open with his teeth and walked it over to her.

From her seat, Celie stopped writhing and began sniffing the air in Michael's direction. When she saw what he was carrying, she whined and struggled to get to it.

"Shh..." He spoke softly to her, desperate to earn her trust. "I've got what you need, love." Then he reached around and gently grabbed the back of her head. Steadying her, he brought the pouch up to her lips, where she ravenously tore into it. Blood splattered across the chair and her face as she dove in, slurping up the contents like a dog that hadn't eaten for days. As she did this, she looked up at Michael and watched him. He smiled softly and stroked her hair, whispering sweet things to her.

From across the room, Kat turned and cried into Xander's chest. Xander welcomed her with open arms.

Chapter Ten

Recovery

On Sunday morning, the vampire came to rest.

Kat had noticed that Celie's ears were starting to recede, her fingernails starting to dwindle down. They were no longer sharp and pointed, no longer claws that could tear apart flesh. Her demand for blood was winding down, too; she was calmer and more aware.

Kat also noticed that Celie was starting to recognize them.

"Here you go, sweetie." Kat handed a pouch of donor blood to Celie. She spent most of her time in the chair in the corner, but that was okay for now. Celie grabbed the pouch from her and proceeded to puncture it with her teeth. However, she began calmly sucking the blood from it, drinking her fill and even smiling as she did so.

Kat was still cautious around Celie, like a rehabber would be around a wild animal. She maintained a safe distance, kept a watchful eye on her, and never let her guard down. It also didn't hurt that no matter what, Xander or Michael (or both) were always there. She had backup to keep things in check if they should get out of hand. Fortunately, that hadn't happened.

Today was different, though. Despite what seemed like a journey into darkness, today Celie was beginning to show signs of returning to herself. The smile that she sent Kat over her drink was the best thing Kat had seen since this whole fiasco, and she turned away to smile at Michael, sitting across the room.

"Do you see this?" Kat didn't dare move for fear she would disturb the moment.

Michael smiled tenderly in response.

Kat turned her attention back to Celie and talked to her. She used calm words, telling her softly and quietly how much they loved her and how much they couldn't wait to have her back. Celie watched Kat with inquisitive eyes and simply smiled as she drank. Once she was done, Celie gingerly relinquished her pouch to Kat. Kat smiled at her and Celie smiled back.

Kat was flying high.

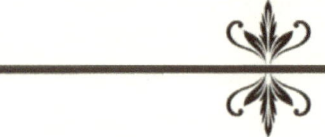

I began to understand these—people?—didn't want to hurt me. I began to understand that they were trying to help me. They provided me with blood, and it satiated me. They gave me shelter, and I was comfortable. They did not smother me or ensnare me, so I was able to breathe. I even started recognizing some of their speech. The woman was very nice, quiet, soft, like a little bird. She fluttered around me and spoke nicely to me. The dark man was also nice to be around, his words sounding like soft rumblings, warm and reassuring.

The other man was hushed, too, keeping his voice low and gentle. But there was something about him, more so than the others, that held my interest. He watched me from across the room, and I held his gaze. After a time, he would look away, but when I did the same, I would always find him staring at me later on. I couldn't imagine why, but there was something protective in his eyes. Appreciating his protection, I found myself smiling at him here and there.

Michael loved seeing a smile on Celie. He loved it more than anything that had ever been or ever would be. Today was a good day, and he was happy that he had been able to bear witness to it.

Standing, Michael stretched, bending his arms backward and arching his back. This strange set of movements caught Celie's attention. She stood up from her chair and watched him. In a form of mimicry, she also stretched, and Michael knew that she was bonding with him. He only hoped it meant that his Celie was soon around the corner...

Three hours later, Celie spoke her first word.

"Home."

Kat spun around from where she was standing talking to Xander. "Oh my god, did you hear that?"

"I sure did." Xander smiled warmly as he looked across the room at Celie. "It's a good sign."

"Are you kidding? It's a fantabulous sign!"

Pulling her phone from her back pocket, she dialed Michael, who had gone out to get more blood pouches from a local hospital. "Michael!... Yes, it's amazing news—she spoke!... Yeah!... 'Home'... Okay, hurry up and get back here, would ya?"

After she had hung up, Kat turned to Xander. "I can't believe she said 'home'. Do you think she means her home with Michael?"

"Most likely. I mean, what else could she mean by it?"

"Well, she could mean her home with me or her home with the little old Irish lady. It's possible she meant either of those, right?"

"It's possible, sure. But we can't put too much intention on one word."

Kat frowned. "Yeah, I'm sure you're right. It's just so amazing!" Kat turned to Celie. "I wonder what's going on in that head of hers..."

I felt like I was waking up from a dream. A very bad dream. Better yet, a nightmare. One in which I had metamorphosed into a giant demon creature and hunted down everyone I loved. No one was safe, and I had lost all control of myself.

I tried to speak, but words felt garbled and uneasy on my tongue. I managed one word: home. I hoped they knew what I meant. I remembered Bantum. I remembered the SpellCasters and what they had done. I wanted to go home with Michael, to get away from this waking nightmare. I needed to be around familiar, comforting things.

I watched everyone move about the room. It was almost like I had suddenly become *aware* of them, as if one moment I was in the dark, seeing nothing but endless black, and the next I was in this room with them milling about. Kat was beaming, and Xander was all smiles.

As I watched them, Michael abruptly appeared to my right. He put some items on a table and took the two additional steps necessary to come over. He knelt down in front of me, reached up, and tucked some stray hairs back behind my right ear. He shared a sweet smile with me, something pleasing him very much, then shared that smile with the others. I wasn't sure what had made them all so happy, but I tried to join in by also smiling.

That merely caused more of the same.

Michael tried to ask me about 'home'. I just looked at him and nodded, hoping he would understand. His voice sounded faint and distant. I touched my own throat and shook my head. He nodded back, as if understanding that I couldn't answer him. Kat and Xander appeared disappointed, but I couldn't appease them. I felt like a disappointment, like I was letting them down.

What had happened to me?

I remembered being in the walled garden with Michael, finally getting my memory back, and then, with no warning, I was here in this hotel room with him, Kat and Xander. At least I was with the people I loved. At least I was safe.

I worried about Fiadh. I hadn't seen her in God knows how long. Had it been hours? Days? Weeks? I didn't know. But I knew that I needed to focus on getting over this...*thing* that had happened to me so I could check on her. She needed someone to look after her.

"Fiadh," I said. It sounded harsh, like my voice box had been plowed down by a freight train and then run through a cement mixer.

Michael started; his eyes wide. He then smiled and nodded once, standing up and walking over to Kat and Xander. He said something to them, after which they grabbed some jackets, smiled at me and left. Kat even threw in a little wave as she walked out the door. All I could do was blink at her in response.

Walking back to the table he'd left things on when he first arrived, Michael picked up a dark red pouch. I immediately knew what it was and began salivating, licking my lips and watching his every move anxiously. He knelt back in front of me, and I managed a whimper. Sorrow filled his face as he tore open the pouch. Handing it to me, I immediately took it from him, and began drinking from it. I felt like I hadn't had any food or sustenance for weeks, and I was so incredibly hungry. I appreciated every ounce that came from the pouch, practically licking it clean, tilting my head back in my efforts to capture every drop.

Once I was done, I lowered my head back down, and Michael was watching me, as he likes to do. I licked my lips clean and wiped my face on the back of my black shirt sleeve. As I handed the pouch back to him, I managed to utter, "Th...thank... ...y...you. Th-thank you, Muh... Mike."

You would have thought that I had been the first woman on the moon; the celebration was so incredible.

Michael grinned so big, and he leaned his head back and laughed heartily, a happy sound that sounded less far away than before. The next thing I knew, he was putting the pouch down and reaching for me. Skittish as I was still feeling, I wasn't afraid of him. I knew him, loved him, and was happy to be back in his arms. He enveloped me and began pressing kisses all over my forehead and face.

I grinned in response, immediately happier that he was with me, and we were together. No more separation. No more distance. No more nightmares. No more lost memories. We were *together*, and it was as if a weight had been lifted off of me. I felt lighter and more positive than I had in forever, more loved than I had any right to be.

I still couldn't manipulate my vocal cords as well as I wanted to. However, it occurred to me that we had another option. Remembering Michael's ability to speak to me inside my head, I reached out to him. My first thoughts were still and quiet, but I projected them as best I could, furrowing my brow in concentration.

Mike... Mike, can you hear me?

Michael leaned back on his haunches and beamed from ear to ear. *There you are, love. Oh lord, it's so good to have you back.*

Am I? I paused. *Am I back?*

Well, you will be in due time.

What...what happened to me?

You don't remember, do you?

No... I... I remember the garden...and it was nighttime...

It's okay. His tone was calm and soothing, and I felt my tension ease. *I can tell you.* He closed his eyes and took a deep breath. Opening his eyes, he looked right into mine. *You went feral.*

Feral? I eyed him quizzically, my brow furrowed again as I tried to understand what he meant.

Yes.

What... What does that mean?

It means that you went into full basic instinct mode. Your body didn't understand why you hadn't fed in so many days and reverted into a primal state of being.

Primal state?

You stopped being Celie and started being a vampire.

My eyes widened as what he was saying sank into my brain. Primal. Vampire. Basic Instinct. All of it sounded foreboding. I had been a vampire for several months now, so I was perplexed about what he meant. *What did I do?*

Well, you ran from me. I tried to get you to drink when you began to change, but you launched me across the garden and took off.

I launched you?

Yes. Your strength was increased, and your instincts were that of an animal.

Oh god...

Michael smirked. *Had nothing to do with it,* he finished. *This was a result of your molecular chemistry struggling to survive. You were literally fighting to exist, battling a hunger that you haven't known before because you hadn't been starving before.*

Has this happened to you before?

Just once, but I had someone to help me out of it, just like we've been doing for you.

I paused, then asked him again what I desperately needed to know. *You didn't answer me, Mike. I can feel it, a feeling that something horrible happened. What did I do?*

Michael paused this time. An expression of struggle was on his face. Something was warring inside of him, and I knew I wasn't going to like what I was about to hear.

Just say it.

Michael sighed and looked down. "You found a house with someone inside. Before I could get to you...you fed on them." With those words, he looked up at me.

I stared into his silver eyes. *Did I... Oh lord... I killed someone...?*

Michael said nothing, his lips tight, his eyes never leaving mine.

With that, I broke down. I began sobbing uncontrollably, pulling my legs up in the chair and wrapping my arms around my knees. I bent my head to the top of my knees and cried heavy, salty tears of grief. I had never killed a living thing before, save for a bug on a windshield. I usually saved crickets and spiders, putting them out of the house gently. I hated snakes, but I had never killed one. The idea that I was responsible for the death of another person was gut-wrenching to me. Did they have a family? What did I force them to leave behind? They must have been terrified by me...

All of these thoughts and more spun around in my head. I clenched my fists, gripping my pants tightly and feeling my nails dig into my palms through the soft cotton fabric. My vision blurred, I looked up at Michael, and he looked as lost as I felt. For a time, we simply sat across from each other, sharing in the heartache.

Michael reached out to me and smoothed my hair back away from my face. His palm was comforting against my face, and I nuzzled into it, eager to feel his touch, his calm during this moment. His hand came down and cupped my cheek, his thumb wiping tears from my face. I looked at him expectantly and swallowed.

I knew what I wanted...

...and I wanted it from him.

Without skipping a heartbeat, I put my legs down and reached out for him. Pulling Michael close, I kissed him, tasting him and inhaling his warm scent. He kissed me back, matching my passion and taming his ferocity; it was in his kiss, his lips, his tongue. I melted against him, loving the feel of my breasts pressed hard against his chest.

His arms came around me and his hands slid down to my waist. Before I knew it, he had pulled me off the chair and onto his lap. Sliding my hands into his unbound hair, I wrapped my legs around him eagerly and pressed my hips into his, gyrating against him and feeling him harden underneath me. With one free hand, I slipped my fingers down his chest and past his waistband until I found my prize. He groaned, and I nipped his lip. I tasted his blood and smiled against his lips.

Whatever he had been holding back was lost. He leaned me back against the chair and pushed my legs toward me. My leggings were torn off of me, leaving me exposed from the waist down. I didn't care. I let him wrap my legs around his waist again, and I leaned forward. Cradling my ass, Michael lowered me onto his cock, and I was filled with him. The sensation of being one with him was nearly too much to bear. I purred for him and he growled, low and deep. His eyes were hooded, blazing with molten heat, and I felt its sear on my heart, on my soul.

I took his mouth with mine, beginning my conquest above and below. My hips moved with a wanton abandon, riding him impatiently, then slowly, then back again. I teased and tortured my lover with my hips and my tongue until I felt him grab me, one of his hands on each hip, and he began to thrust urgently, moving us faster, harder. Each thrust was reckless abandon. Each movement was one step closer to the edge, until...

I broke free of my earthly bonds, and I screamed his name in my mind. I heard my own name echo there, and we collapsed in each other's arms, panting. His hands stroked my hair, and I continued to kiss him softly, completely spent.

After a time, my lust and need for him satiated, I let him carry me to the bed and cover me with a blanket. I kissed him tenderly, then I turned on my side. I felt the bed sink slightly as he climbed onto it, curling up behind me, a slight creak coming from the bed frame. Once his arms were around me, I was only too happy to sleep.

Chapter Eleven

Arrangements

"We need Ricky's help."

"Why?"

"We need to know what we're up against. Maybe he can look up some lore or something that we can't access here."

Kat looked pensive. "Ok, I suppose that would be alright. I just hate involving anyone who doesn't need to be involved."

"I know, but we need to stop these people, and the more intel we have, the better."

"Agreed." Michael walked up to my side. He put his hand on my lower back, and I smiled inwardly at the sensation of his touch.

Xander sat in one of the room's chairs. He looked scholarly, wearing a gray knit sweater and well-pressed khaki pants. A silver chain peeked out from the top of his sweater as he leaned forward, his elbows on his knees. "As much as we want to protect him, Kat, we need his help."

Kat nodded; a bit sorrowful but resigned. She pulled out her phone and found where she had dialed Ricky those few days previous. She hit the dial button and put it on speakerphone.

"Ricky here..."

I leaned forward. "Hey Ricky."

"Red! How the hell are ya? We were all super worried about you!"

I smiled. "Thanks, Ricky. I'm doing okay now. I heard you helped find me?"

"You bet I did! I'm glad Kat reached out to me."

"I'm hoping you can help us again. Are you free?"

"Absolutely! What's up?"

I looked up at Michael, whose face was stern and determined. "Well, I'm going to be straight up with you–"

"Please do."

"We're being hunted." I actually wanted to laugh a little at the absurdity of it all.

"Um...say what now?"

"The whole reason I went missing, and Kat reached out to you for help, is because we were attacked by these people who want to kill us."

"Get the fuck out. Who are they? Why do they want to kill you?"

"Long story, but we need your help looking up information about them."

"Yeah. Yeah! Of course! But I need some more background. What info do you already have on them?"

"Well, I guess the long story is going to be a short story. Okay...Um, are you sitting down?" I looked around at Kat and Xander, who each nodded at me in agreement.

"Uh, yeah, I guess so. Why? Is this going to make me freak out?"

"I don't know."

"C'mon then, just spit it out."

I inhaled and then blurted the big secret out. "I'm a vampire. The people after me and Michael, my boyfriend, are vampire hunters, and they can use magic."

Ricky snorted. "Is this a joke?"

"Nope. No joke."

"Oh c'mon. You've gotta be pulling my leg or something."

"Ricky, I'm serious. Serious as a heart attack."

Ricky paused for a minute, then began laughing. "I just..." More laughter. "I just can't believe you think I don't know about this shit."

"What!" Kat, Xander, and Michael all stared at the phone. "What the hell do you mean, you 'know about this shit'?"

Ricky continued laughing, then managed to speak in between bursts of amusement. "Because I'm one of them."

"One what?"

"Oh lordy, girl. A vampire!"

"Get the fuck outta here..." Now it was my turn to be incredulous, with all of us standing around looking shocked. This was definitely news to each of us.

"No, I'm serious!"

I was flabbergasted. I had no idea. No inkling. There was nothing on the radar to indicate that Ricky was a vampire...except... Except that he was a terribly smart, ridiculously bright individual who was already making hand over fist at the tender age of 17. And we never met his parents.

And he never seemed to look any older than 20.

I managed to pick my jaw up from off the ground and close it. "You're a vampire?"

"Yeah, girl."

"How the hell did I miss that?" Kat was now sitting on the floor. Ricky's news had sent her to the ground, fainting dead away. Xander had gotten to her pretty quickly, catching her before she hit her head, then waking her up so she wouldn't miss anything. He was kneeling next to her and shaking his head in befuddled amusement. I'm not sure anything was surprising to him anymore.

"Hey Katie-Kat! You know? I don't know. I never really figured out how to hide it, other than hiding myself every 20 or 25 years odd years or so. Then I have to start over somewhere else."

Michael nodded in understanding.

"Did you know about this?"

"Me? No, I had no idea about Ricky, but it makes sense."

"Have you ever met other vampires aside from Amelia?"

Michael nodded again. I guess I had a few things to learn. I turned my attention back to the phone. "So do you know about these SpellCasters, Ricky? Cause if they're after us, they'll be after you soon enough."

"Yeah, I've heard of them. Bad mofos."

"What do you know?"

"I know that you're on the wrong side of that equation and really need some help."

"So help us out." I was getting frustrated.

"I will, but what are you looking for, exactly?"

"History on these guys. Details that might give us clues on how we can get rid of them."

"Let me see what I can dig up. I can tell you that the fact that you've survived this long is a good sign for you, but bad in the grand scheme of things."

"Bad why?"

"Bad because they aren't done with you."

Running.
Faster. Harder. Stronger.

Day and night, we are running.

But it never seems to be enough. Could never be enough. The SpellCasters are close behind. We don't know how they found us. We don't know how much longer we will remain alive.

Elena and I are desperate to survive. We've been hiding for months now, but the SpellCasters continue to track us. We don't know how. No matter what abilities we use or don't use, they seem to know exactly where we are and how to locate us. Nothing seems able to protect us.

Elena is ready to give up. I tell her not to, that we will make it, that we will find a way to outrun them. There has to be a way to outwit them.

And yet...

Everything I have heard over the years has told me that the SpellCasters are doom incarnate. Vampires everywhere should live in fear of them and do live in fear of them. Their magic uses the elements and combines those powers to create death and destruction for us all. Nothing can combat it.

Nothing.

Elena is scared. I am scared. We've made our way to Boston in the hopes that a larger city might make it more difficult to track us. Hiding in large numbers, as it were. I have some old colony members that may be able to help us. Perhaps one of them knows more about the SpellCasters. Their history is vast, and their reach is great. But hopefully we can learn something to enable us to put up a fight.

I can only hope we survive the night.

X Stephan X

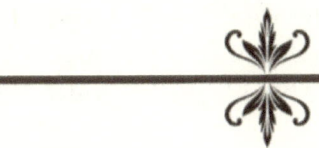

I sat back from the computer. Ricky had located an archive of vampire lore on a black site. I had just read the last letter about the

SpellCasters, documented by a vampire named Stephan. It seemed Stephan didn't escape their clutches either.

None of this bodes well.

I closed the laptop and turned to Michael. "We're in for some serious hurt."

"You don't say."

I looked over at Kat and Xander. "You two shouldn't be involved. I want you two to both go home."

"But—"

I interrupted Xander, despite his determined look to help. "But nothing. This is our fight. They don't want you, and as far as I'm concerned, they never will. Let's keep you out of this. Go home."

"I really don't think—"

"I love you both. We both do." I gestured between myself and Michael. "So please—go home."

Resigned, Xander stepped back, but Kat looked pissed. "How dare you..."

"Ah shit... Here we go again," mumbled Xander.

"You think we would fly to Ireland to come looking for you if it wasn't our fight, too? That's just low."

"I meant no disrespect, Kat—"

"You sure as hell sound it."

"I'm just worried about you."

"And we were worried about you, but we tracked you down, and we came all the way here."

"I would never forgive myself if something happened to you."

"That's just some selfish shit. Where do you get off shoving us away when you're about to face off with the big bads? Hmm? That's some bullshit."

"We only want you both to be safe."

"We may not be directly impacted by this shit you're in, but your fight is our fight, too." She threw up a well-known hand gesture. "And fuck you if you don't like it."

I couldn't help it. I laughed. "Good lord, I love you so much Kat." I walked over to her and helped her up. Despite her glare, I gave her a huge hug. She hugged me back, and when she pulled away, her glare had finally gone.

"I still don't want you here when they get here."

"But I—"

"You're too damn important to me."

Kat's glare was back, and she lowered her eyes. If her being safe meant she would be mad at me, that was okay. I could live with that—I couldn't live with her death.

"Xander, can you please book some flights for you guys to head home?"

"I'm on it." Xander reached around me and grabbed the laptop.

Before he could pass me, I stayed his hand. "Wait." I turned my attention back to Kat. "You wanna help?"

"Of course." She growled at me, still perturbed.

"How about going to Boston."

Kat perked up. "Boston?"

"Yeah. I'm thinking that maybe you could do some digging into local vampire colonies. Maybe drag Ricky with you? You know, for validity's sake."

Kat turned to look at Xander. He shrugged his shoulders, apparently okay with the idea. Kat turned back to me, thoughtful in her gaze. "Okay, we'll fly to Boston and see what we can find out." She poked me in the chest. "But this doesn't mean you can leave us out of the loop. You better keep us posted on anything you find out, anything you encounter."

"Scout's honor."

"I mean it. If they show up, you better let me or Xander know. No hiding things. I was serious when I said, 'your fight is our fight, too.'"

"I swear, Kat."

She hugged me, and I smiled over her shoulder at Xander, who looked relieved the 'fight' was over. I hated fighting with her, but she was as stubborn as an ox. I figured if she wanted to be part of this, I could at least keep her as far away from it as possible.

Once she pulled away, I turned to Michael. "We need to get prepared for them."

"We do."

"But first, I need to see Fiadh."

"Of course. Let's go see her."

Kat chimed in. "We checked on her for you yesterday. She's doing okay."

"Thanks, but I'd feel better seeing her...and saying goodbye."

I glanced at Michael, and his smile was kind. He knew this wouldn't be easy for me, but he knew that I'd see her again one day. I just hoped it was sooner rather than later.

Michael and I left the hotel in the SUV and rode through town, turning northeast towards Fiadh's home. When we arrived, there was an air about the house that spoke of magic. Not the sparkly kind that leaves you feeling like you walked into a strawberry-scented glitter bomb. Oh no. This was the kind that left you with goosebumps and hairs standing up on the back of your neck. This was dark magic that surrounded the property.

As we pulled into the driveway, Seamus didn't come out to greet us.

The cows were not in the pasture.

The ponies were on the far end of the field, almost as if they were avoiding the house at all costs—within their realm of control. They whinnied to me from across the grass but stayed away. Their movements were skittish and anxious.

This was not good.

I closed the SUV door behind me and approached the house quickly, urgently, with Michael at my heels. I reached the front door and didn't bother knocking. I turned the doorknob and barged in, eager to find Fiadh and make sure she was okay. I moved fast through the downstairs rooms until I reached the kitchen.

She was sitting at the small table. Her brown shawl was comfortably draped around her shoulders, and her hands were around her teacup. Steam was still rising from its contents.

Nevertheless, her eyes were blank, lifeless, veiled. There was no light left within her. My beloved Irish matriarch was gone.

I burst into hysterics, crying and sobbing for the loss of another person. Fiadh was more than a kind woman. I had only been a few days in her company, but she had been like a grandmother to me. I ached for her spirited words and her smile. Instead, I was again being assaulted with death and loss.

"Why?" I sobbed. "Why does this keep happening?"

I felt Michael's hand on my shoulder. I turned into him, reaching inside his gray jacket to grab his white shirt, pulling and clutching at it in misery as I cried into his chest. His arms came around me as I continued to shed my tears, my breath catching on each rise of pain and heartache in my chest. I felt him kiss the top of my head and rest his cheek there.

My tears of mourning seemed to have no end. "I hope it was quick," I whispered, my words muffled against him.

All of a sudden, Michael stiffened. "It was also recent." He shoved me back and gripped my upper arms, staring down into my eyes. "We need to go. *Now*."

Oh shit, I thought. He was right; the tea was still warm. They could not have been here more than fifteen minutes ago. We had to vacate the premises—stat.

I turned to look at Fiadh one more time, my eyes blurring with more tears. I expressed my goodbyes, silent, unspoken, but heartfelt.

137

Then I took Michael's hand and followed him back through the house, rushing toward the front door.

One hand on his arm, I squeezed him to get him to look at me. "We can't let them find Kat and Xander."

"I know."

We hurried to the SUV and got in, Michael quickly starting the car. That was when I noticed it: a baby blue vehicle with tail fins idling up the road from the house. I grabbed Michael's arm, unable to tear my attention away, letting him follow my gaze to see what had urgently caught my attention. He growled low in his throat, and I looked to see his expression had turned into one of rage, his eyes dark and stormy. Hurriedly, he shifted gears and hit reverse, throwing the SUV backwards. I braced myself against the dashboard and passenger door, vibing hard with his urgency and feeling my anxiety skyrocketing. Michael barely used the brake as he shifted into drive and hit the gas pedal, jerking me in my seat and speeding out onto the road. As he drove, I used the side mirror to monitor our escape.

It wasn't working very well.

"Let's hurry this thing up, Mike."

"I'm working on it." His face serious, his expression grim. I saw him look in the rearview mirror. He was watching them, too.

I whipped out my phone and immediately called Xander, fingers clumsily dialing as I felt panic rising within me.

"Get out. Get out now."

"Why? What's going on?"

"They're coming. We're going to try to lead them away, but you need to go. *Go now*."

"Understood. We'll call when we're in Boston."

"Be careful."

With that, I hung up. I looked over at Michael. "I love you."

He set his sights on me momentarily. "I love you, too."

We were silent for a minute or two. "This isn't the end for us. Not by a long shot. You and I have survived so much worse than this."

I smiled weakly. "I know. I just don't know how we're going to make it through."

"By staying together. I have a plan."

"Oh? Care to share with the class?"

"Once we've reached a safe distance, we're going to ditch the car, and I'll take us somewhere far away."

"So we're...what? Going to bounce around from place to place?" I glanced in my own mirror and saw that—albeit smaller than before—the blue car was still following us.

"It's temporary, until we can think of something better." He glanced at me. "Unless you had something better in mind?"

I placed a hand on his arm again. "No, no, I like it. We'll be the literal version of Pong. We could start a podcast: 'Globetrotting adventures with Mike and Celie.'"

Michael bowled me over with a smile, and I felt my anxiety wash away. I loved when he smiled. My heart would have had him smile at me all the time, but that was a bit much to ask from a nearly 300-year-old vampire. I mean, what vampire do you know that's all 'sunshine and rainbows'? No, I would take what I could get, and when I could get it. When he smiled, I would relish every second.

"Where to first, then?"

"What were you thinking, Ms. Globetrotter?"

"I'm thinking... Oh! How's Norway this time of year?"

"Chilly."

"I've always wanted to see the fjords... You know, I may have Viking blood in me?"

"Is that a fact...?" Michael continued to smile for me. I still saw him glance in the rearview mirror.

"How much further? I'm ready to end this joyride."

"Almost there." By this time, we had been driving down backroad after backroad, taking side roads and turns here and there. I couldn't see the SpellCasters anymore, but Michael's vision had always been so much better than mine, even after I had turned.

We pulled into a scenic spot overlooking a creek. Michael put the car into park and turned towards me. His eyes were molten silver, bright and fiery just for me. He reached out his hands, and I took them in mine, squeezing his fingers as he ran his thumb over my knuckles. Then I nodded, and he ported us out of the front seat and away into the unknown.

Ionsáiteán

Outrun

"Well, that's just fecking great." Brigit was determined to express her frustrations. "We had them, an' now they've gone an' fecking disappeared." She squirmed in the passenger seat of their vehicle.

From the backseat, Rusalka shared a cheeky little smile. She hated the vampires, as all SpellCasters did, but she hated Brigit just as much, ever since Brigit had nearly killed her one hundred years ago. Seeing her like this was a bright spot in her day.

"Whatever will we do...?" Rusalka feigned fright from her seat, and promptly followed it with childish giggling.

Brigit turned around and slapped her. Hard. A red splotch quickly spread across Rusalka's pale face. In turn, Rusalka screeched loudly and reached out, grabbing Brigit's red hair. She yanked and pulled, instigating retaliation from Brigit, who took handfuls of Russlka's long silvery mane into her clutches. High-pitched screaming took over the once quiet car.

"*Paryaapt!*" From the driver's seat, Pavan twisted his fingers into a set of shapes and unleashed a mini tornado on the two banshees with him. Once they were broken free of each other, the twister dissipated.

Pavan eyed both of them, his face stern and serious. "Are you done behaving like children?"

Brigit and Rusalka sat back in their respective seats, pouting.

Pavan turned his attention back to the field in front of him. Minutes ago, they had caught up to the SUV and pulled over alongside it, but the vampires weren't inside. Pavan was already frustrated with this cockamamy plan Brigit had come up with, but losing his quarrie was something he simply could not take. Combine that with the immature behavior of his compatriots, and he felt like he was losing his mind. He closed his eyes and took several deep breaths, exhaling to a count of ten, and chanting his mantra silently within: *Pavitr maan mujh par najar.* (Sacred mother, watch over me).

Opening his eyes, Pavan surveyed the field for a moment before putting the car in reverse. Once he was back on the road, he began breathing normally. He focused on the drive but realized he needed to come up with a plan for capturing these vampire 'outlaws'.

"We need to find them. We don't know where they have gone, so I recommend one of you scry or use the board."

Brigit was still sulking in the passenger seat and refused to look at him. Rusalka huffed but proceeded to lay out a pendulum board on the backseat. He caught glimpses of her scrying with her sterling silver and aquamarine pendulum, her face scrunched up in intense focus for a few minutes before eventually expressing consternation at the results.

"Um...you're not going to like this." Rusalka's voice was hushed, small.

"What is it?"

"They're not in Roscommon anymore."

"So where are they?"

"It looks like...Norway?"

Pavan hit the brakes, and the car jerked to a halt. He swung around to stare at her. "Norway?"

"That's what the scrying says..."

He swiveled back and eyeballed Brigit. "Norway."

Brigit snorted. She knew this could happen and found it slightly amusing. A chase. How quaint. She hadn't had a good chase in years, so this would be refreshing. She reached out and smacked the dashboard with both hands. "I love it. Let's go!"

"To Norway?"

"Yes, to Norway! We still have to dispatch 'em, don't we?"

Pavan sighed. "Yes. I just didn't want to have to travel that far north."

"Why? What's the big deal?"

Rusalka had to share her opinion, too, and oddly enough, it matched Brigit. "Yeah, what's the big deal with Norway?"

"Nothing." He was not happy about visiting a cold climate. "Okay fine. Shall I take us there, or are we traveling commercially?"

"Ooh, can we take a flight?" Rusalka shimmied forward to grip the back of the front seat. "I haven't flown on a plane in *so long*... And they give you those little bottles with the spirits in them!"

"Fine, we'll get plane tickets." Pavan raised an eyebrow at Brigit. "I'm surprised that you're not angry about this."

"Me? Angry? Whatever for?"

"Because they escaped."

"Oh dear, sweet Pavan... Not to worry. I plan on capturing them." She chuckled with delight. "Capturing them and dismembering them..."

Brigit's fingertips lit up from within. Rolling down the passenger window, she pointed her right hand out in the shape of a gun. As they drove by a piece of farmland, she pretended to fire the 'gun', and a tiny fireball burst forth from her fingertip into a hay roll. Flames came to life within the hay, leaving a trail of smoke to rise into the sky.

She turned to Pavan and smiled. "They won't escape us. Not this time."

Chapter Twelve

The Northern Way

"We're here." Michael released me, and I opened my eyes.

We were standing atop lush, green grass adjacent to the still and blue-green waters of a fjord. Windswept steel gray and icy white mountains towered around us, their heights leaving me feeling incredibly small and awe filled. Clouds grazed the mountain tops and swam lazily through the crisp, cold air. The hint of firewood lingered on the wind. Behind us were rich conifer trees and stark deciduous ones.

His porting capability clearly knew no limits.

It was daytime, and I still held Michael's hands. I closed my mouth, which had been agape while surveying my surroundings, and looked up at my vampire. "'Here' is wondrous."

I smiled for him and let go of his hands to clasp my arms around him. Turning my head to the side, I laid it against his chest as he held me. We stood there for a moment, with me listening to the sounds of nature and feeling his warm body next to mine. I felt like I had arrived in a dream, one I never wanted to wake up from. How was this my life? How did I manage to be in this place, in this moment, with this man—this vampire?

Despite everything we had been through, despite all of our trials and tribulations, I felt blessed.

Well, except where the SpellCasters were concerned—that was more like a curse.

The dreaded arrival of the SpellCasters was something I could do without. Who knew when they would show up. Would it be days? Weeks? Minutes? None of our options were good, in my opinion. Knowing they were inevitable, a mere fact waiting to happen, put a damper on my happy hour—something I was determined to avoid.

I pulled back from Michael. "Kiss me." He leaned down and did just that, his warm lips caressing mine at first, then more passionately as I returned his touch with eagerness. His tongue did incredible things that I couldn't wait to feel more of later. I reached up and threw my arms around his neck, not wanting to part from him. His muscular arms encircled me tighter, and I relished the sensation of being held by him, not wanting the moment to end. Yet all good things...

"You're the best part of my life," I murmured against his mouth.

"You're the best part of my everything," he replied, his lips curving into a smile against mine.

"I never want to lose you," I whispered.

"You won't. Not if I have anything to say about it."

A chill swept through me, and I wasn't sure if it was the cold climate or a sense of impending doom. I glanced around looking for trouble and was happy to find none. It was definitely time for a stiff drink.

"Let's figure out where we are, and then we're finding the nearest pub." I sighed again, but heavily. "It's been a long day."

Suddenly a voice piped up to the right of me. "I can tell ye where ye are, *cailin*. Easily, too, so we can get ye to that pub!"

I knew that voice. I turned to find my lovely, wonderful, decidedly *deceased* Fiadh Murphy standing not seven feet away from me. She was as plain as day, although slightly hazy in the overcast light, and her eyes were as sparkly as ever. Her smile was bright, reaching from ear to ear, and I was delighted to see her looking so happy.

"Fiadh!" I rushed over to her, screeching to a halt just before I would have passed through her misty frame. "My god, woman! I can't believe you're here!"

"Here and t'ere, anyway." Her expression turned to one of sadness, and she seemed to dim slightly, her form appearing more obscure and transparent. "I'm sorry I wasn't able to say goodbye, *cailín*."

I felt tears brimming in my eyes and shook my head. "You're here now, and that's all that matters." I smiled for her, and she brightened, taking on a more solid shape again.

"So ye want to know where ye are?"

"Yes, please!" I turned and reached out for Michael. He walked over to me, taking my hand, then we both gave our full attention to Fiadh. "Sorry! This is Michael."

"Hello, t'ere, Mr. Michael."

In response, Michael gave her a small bow, and Fiadh was delighted and—perhaps—smitten.

"He's my..." I glanced at him and raised one of my eyebrows. "Boyfriend actually sounds weird, now that I think about it."

He pressed a kiss to my forehead. "We'll figure that out later."

With a grin, I looked at my sweet, dear Mrs. Murphy. "We know we're in Norway, but we're not sure just *where* in Norway we are?"

"Geiranger."

"Gah...what now?"

"Geiranger. Well, this is actually Geirangerfjord, but the town not far from here is Geiranger."

"Great!" I laughed and looked over at Michael on my left. "We're not lost!"

"That *is* good news." He laughed along with me.

"Ye'll be heading down that way," said Fiadh, pointing behind us, "about four miles or so. T'ere's a small pub t'ere you'll both enjoy."

"That sounds heavenly. A bit of a walk, but we can manage." I smiled and hoped she knew how much I loved her. "I miss you..." I began to sniffle.

"I miss ye, too, darlin.'"

"Oh Fiadh, is there any way I can repay you?" I wanted to help her in any way imaginable. She had done so much for me, and I felt an obligation to her. "I'm not sure if there's anything you need, or that I can even provide, but if there is, you've got it."

"Oh, yer a sweetheart, ye are. I've got my Connor now. It's all I ever wanted after he was gone. To have him back, that's enough."

"That's brilliant, Fiadh. I'm so thrilled for you," I said through happy tears. I felt Michael's arm come around my shoulders, appreciating his comforting strength.

"Ye won't be forgettin' me now, will ye?"

"Never. You'll be with me, always."

"T'ere's a lass. Now away with ye. Go get that drink and make sure ye be toasting me a time er two."

"Oh, you can count on it, love."

With that, Fiadh smiled and faded into the light of day.

I looked at Michael and grinned, knowing my eyes were glassy with unshed tears. I felt one break free and begin a slow descent down my cheek. Michael reached up and brushed it away with his thumb, smiling back at me.

"Okay, let's head down the way." With that, we began our trek towards the town.

Arriving in Geiranger, we were immediately taken with the quaint little town. It was small, clean, and downright bristling with tourists, but we didn't care about that last bit; it was perfectly adorable. Colorful colors adorned many of the buildings, a stark contrast to the green mountainside. There were tiny souvenir shops, camping signs, and several hotels overlooking the fjord. We headed to one that clearly said it had both a restaurant and bar.

Inside Grønn Utsikt Hotel, the design was very simplistic, full of clean lines with occasional touches of old world charm: colorful tiles, decorative chandeliers, etc. The colors were comfortable warm neutrals, with some blues here and there. Sunlight streamed in through the large glass doors and windows lining the front wall of the lobby.

Michael and I approached reception and greeted the desk clerk, booking a room overlooking the fjord. We were given a room on the third of four floors, with a balcony and private bathroom. The receptionist told us the room had a large, walk-in shower, and I groaned at the idea of hot water.

"*Tusen takk*," said the clerk after we paid for our room. They gave us directions to it and provided us with basic instructions on when dinner was served, when the bar was open, and so on. We thanked them, and the clerk gave a traditional reply, "*Vær så god*."

Once we were done, Michael and I headed upstairs. After hiking four miles, we were ready to unwind, so we took the elevator. Reaching the third floor, we found our room and went inside, Michael closing the door behind us. I walked over to the balcony to stare at the breathtaking view.

"Have you ever seen anything this beautiful before?" I was unable to take my eyes off the fjord and valley shore. The mountains rose up high on either side, like protective walls around a precious gem. The clouds danced across the sky, sunlight dappling the landscape. I was in awe.

"Yes, I have." I sensed Michael's approach behind me. I turned to meet him, smiling. "You," he continued, his voice low and deep, the barest hint of a growl gilding it.

"Me?" I feigned innocence.

He smirked. "You know how gorgeous you are." He leaned forward, placing his hands on the railing on each side of me. He was staring at me, hunger in his eyes, and I felt the heat pouring off of him like lava. Butterflies began to rattle around inside me—only he could do that to me everytime—and I knew what was coming. "You're the most beautiful thing I've ever seen."

His head bent close, and he pressed a kiss to my collarbone, his lips warm and soft. A second later, his tongue was gliding up my neck, and he nipped me. I couldn't help my sharp inhale, and I slid my fingers into his hair. He moved up until he was hovering just over my mouth.

"You keep doing things like that," I whispered, "and I'll throw you on that bed and rip your clothes off."

"Mmm, is that so?" he murmured. I nodded, and he said, "Well, as brilliant an idea as that is, I have a different idea you might love just as much."

"Oh?"

Admiring the view could wait.

We stripped each other bare, kissing and touching each other in ways that only heightened our arousal for each other. We made our way into the private bath, and while waiting for the water to warm up, we stood on the tiles, letting the chill of the air caress our skin. He dove in, kissing my neck again before working his way down to my breasts, capturing one nipple with his mouth and the other with his fingers as I scratched my nails down his back. I reached up and took his hair out of the leather wrap it was in, letting it fall to his shoulders.

I moved him away, holding him back by his muscular arms and admiring just how damn handsome he was.

"What is it?" His deep voice sent chills over my naked flesh. His silver eyes were blazing and flickering as he watched me.

"How did I get to be so lucky?"

He grinned, but it was delicious. "Oh no, love," he pulled me close again. "I'm the lucky one."

I took his face in my hands and kissed him. His hands found my ass and squeezed. I pressed myself closer to him, aching for whatever he could (and would) willingly give me.

The water grew hot, steam pouring into the space we occupied. He stepped inside the shower and held my hand as I followed. We each relished the feel of warm, clean water as it ran over our bodies. Michael caressed my skin, sliding a single hand from my neck down the middle of my breasts and over my belly, then further still until he could slip his wet fingers inside of me.

I arched my back, closing my eyes and grabbing his hand, urging him onward. He leaned into me, letting some of his weight push his fingers deeper. Michael put his forehead to mine, exhaling a breath against my face as he thrust his fingers inside of me again and again. He used his thumb to unravel me, encircling my clit until I was whimpering. I urged him on, rubbing against him and moaning for more.

I felt him smile, heard him whisper for me to let go, and then he began to move faster, more deliberately. My breathing grew frantic as I felt my body begin to climb higher, my hips moving in time with his motions. Suddenly it was as if sunshine had broken through the clouds and shone directly into my soul. Shards of piercing light enveloped me, and I shimmered. My body clenched around his fingers, and he groaned with delight at my pleasure. Shuddering, my breath caught, and I opened my eyes, anxious to see his own. Without a doubt, my vampire had the sexiest, most seductive gaze on the planet. I clenched against him as he withdrew his fingers, then watched as he slowly brought them up to his mouth. I couldn't help but bite my lip as I watched him suck my juices from his fingertips.

He smiled at me, and I saw a bit of fang. I melted instantly, kissing him ferociously out of desperation to have more of him. Once I felt him sliding his hands down my hips, I pulled back and gave him an eyebrow.

"Tsk-tsk. Now it's my turn..." I put a finger to his lips before he could contradict me. Keeping my eyes on his, I slid down his frame, my hands gliding along his silky, wet, muscular body. I stopped to kiss his navel, feeling him stiffen in anticipation of where I was headed. His hands went to my head, and I felt his fingers slide into my hair and he took a handful in his fist.

Ah...right where I wanted him...

I shifted my focus to what was directly in front of me, sliding further down, intermittently placing feather-light kisses. I licked a trail down his taut belly until I reached the length of him. My hands had been following along his sides, but now I was going to put them to use. I reached forward and gently wrapped one of my hands around his rock hard cock, lightly squeezing. I looked up and saw his head was tilted back, his eyes closed, his mouth slightly open.

Mmm...Good...

I leaned forward and put just the tip of him inside my mouth, enveloping him with my warmth and my lips. I heard him exhale again, a slight moan escaping his lips, and I couldn't help but smile against him. My tongue stroked him inside my mouth, and I leaned forward to take more of him in. His hands clenched my hair harder, and I felt him stretch against my lips. I began to move my mouth over him, my tongue stroking the underside of his shaft, sucking on him like the hard candy that he was. His breathing grew faster, and I felt him tighten again. I knew he was close—a soft whimper escaped him. I still had my hand wrapped around the base of his shaft, and I squeezed, holding him tighter. I pulled back and licked the tip of him, then slid my mouth over him again and again. Just when I thought he couldn't take any more, I flicked my tongue over the underside of his cock. He emptied himself into me, groaning and gasping as he held my head still. Once he was spent, I gently slid my mouth off of him, swallowing and smiling.

I stood up and Michael simply stood there with his head tilted back, eyes closed, breathing heavily. When he finally brought his head down to look at me, his eyes were brilliant—vibrant and stunning—like stars that could burn a hole through the very core of me. I inhaled but never exhaled, feeling my breath catch in my throat.

How did I come to deserve this incredible man in my life?

Michael's eyes pierced mine, and he gently leaned in, kissing me softly and tenderly. His lips were rich, wet from the shower. When he pulled back, I licked my own lips, and he smiled.

"There has never been anyone like you, Celie—*ever*—and I pray I never have to rediscover life without you."

In the steam of the shower, water pouring over us, I took his face in my hands. I stroked his left cheek with my thumb and stared deep into his eyes. Stretching up to kiss him, my lips lingered for a moment.

"I never knew our love was possible. This—what we have—this is everything." Looking down, I placed my hands on his chest. After a moment, I looked back up into his eyes. "You are my world, Michael. Everything would mean nothing without you. No matter what we've been through, no matter what is coming—all I want is what I have right now with you."

Michael pressed a kiss to my forehead as he drew me into his arms. I pressed kisses to his shoulder as he caressed my back. We stayed like that for a time, letting the water envelop us, washing away the past. Even if for a short time, we were simply together.

Eventually we collected ourselves and finished up in the shower, taking turns washing each other's hair. Outside of the shower, we dried off and climbed into bed together. Michael lay on his back, and I nestled against his side, laying my head in the crook of his arm. We lay still and quiet, falling asleep in each other's arms.

In the morning, we woke up, got dressed, and went searching for a local hospital or clinic. I was still in recovery, so Michael was anxious that we acquire blood. I definitely agreed. We also had to find more clothes, but one thing at a time. Our current clothes would do for the moment.

The clerk at the front desk greeted us warmly. "*God morgen.*"

"God morgen." I understood a 'good morning' when I heard it. Many years of foreign language classes in high school came in handy now and then.

"How can I help?" The clerk this morning was a young man with short brown hair and bright blue eyes. His face had a genuine smile, accentuated by his round cheeks. His skin was pale, borderline alabaster, and he had tattoos creeping out from beneath his sleeves. I smiled at my fellow tattoo lover.

"We were hoping we could locate a local hospital or clinic?"

"Oh my. Are you hurt? Should I call a *doktor*?"

"Oh no, no. We're just fine. But I need a prescription for a medicine I take back in the states. Can you help us?"

"Of course. Just head out the doors and go right. Follow the road down the hill until you reach the town, then make another right onto *Sommerfugl Gate*. Keep walking until you see the *sykehus*."

"Tusen takk." I was pretty sure I was thanking him.

"Vær så god," came his response along with another smile.

We followed his directions and made our way through town to the hospital. On arrival, I sat on a bench outside while Michael went in. He was the one who carried the medical card and had the connections for acquiring the blood donations. On second thought, I realized I couldn't rely on him all the time and it might be best for me to get my own. I'd have to talk with him about this once we got home.

Home. It had been so long since I was there, and I couldn't wait to return. Being in foreign countries was amazing, full of sights and sounds that a year ago I would have never thought possible. However, these were circumstances I would have just as soon avoided at all costs. Still, I could dream of being home, safe and sound in our own bed or watching a sunset with a glass of Pinot Noir.

The bench I was on was freezing. I shivered, rubbing my hands together and tucking them between my thighs, then I looked around, watching various Norwegian citizens and tourists passing me by. I wondered how many of them lived here? Worked here? How many of them knew how beautiful this cold place was? How lucky they are to enjoy this view every day? I hoped they did, hoped they had an inkling of what I knew sitting there on that icy bench. Maybe one day I would return to Norway, to these fjords and mountains. Maybe one day Michael and I would make this our home.

One day...

After a time, I saw Michael exit the hospital's main doors, hearing the subtle hiss as they automatically slid closed behind him. He grinned and held up a freezer pouch. I immediately felt myself salivate, knowing what was inside the bag. As he approached, I stood up, ready to seize the bag from him.

"Not here."

"Right, right." I shook my head. "Of course."

"Let's take this back to the hotel, then we'll get you taken care of."

"I'm glad they didn't give you a hard time." We began to walk back in the direction of Grønn Utsikt.

"Likewise. I hate to think about the alternative."

"Me, too." I took his hand and held it in both of mine as we walked. "I don't want a repeat performance of Ireland."

Michael squeezed my hands. "Never. It will never happen again, I promise you." He looked down at me, concern on his face. "Actually, your hands are pretty cold. Are you hungry?"

"Famished, actually."

"No problem. Let's go check this spot out over here."

We left the beaten path and walked off into the conifer trees to share a meal together.

Chapter Thirteen

Ta En Drink På Meg

Sitting with my sixth glass of whiskey was a delight. In fact, I closed my eyes and 'mmm'd' after swallowing the potent spirit, enjoying the fiery burn as it traveled down my throat and into my belly. As a vampire, alcohol didn't have the same 'hit' that it did when I was human. It took a bit more to feel the tingly start of getting swacked; thus, drinking was a touch more expensive now.

I leaned cozily back into my chair, feeling the warmth spread through me. My new clean clothes—a pair of jeans, a white vintage t-shirt with the Queen logo on it, and gray boots—were feeling extra comfortable. When I opened my eyes, Michael was looking pensive, his eyes staring just beyond me, clearly miles away. I put down my glass and outstretched my hand to touch his own. He shook himself out of the cloud he was in and gave me a very weak smile. I squeezed his hand.

"What is it?"

He let out a breath. "I can never hide my anxiety with you, can I?"

"Not on your life, mister."

He chuckled. Looking down at his glass, his brow furrowed. "We still don't know how we're going to win against them." He looked back up into my eyes. "How we're going to fight them... How we can ensure the outcome is on our side..."

"We know we can accomplish anything as long as we're together," I said confidently. I smacked his hand and leaned back in my chair, ice clinking in my glass. "SpellCasters be damned. We can do anything and everything."

"I'm serious, Celie."

"So am I! Don't you for a minute doubt that we can win."

"I do, though. They have spells, magic that we don't possess."

"But you have your demons, and I have my transformation skills—"

"Demons helped me with Meyana, but your transformation abilities did little to help out before."

"Oh... Her name was Meyana, eh?" I mentally switched gears as I was sideswiped by the slut train. "And just how long did it take for the demons to help you out, again? Hmm?"

"Please, not now." He lowered his voice, and I wondered if he was concerned I would get rowdy in the bar.

"Well, I can't bloody help it!" I didn't care that my jealousy was rearing its fat ugly head. I may not have blamed him for what happened, but that didn't mean I wasn't still upset that it happened at all. "I don't know how long you were with her, and it still hurts to think about it." I sniffled.

"I know it does, but damn it, Celie," he ground out from behind his fangs. "Let's not make a scene."

"Oh, fuck your ancient etiquette."

Uh-oh, I was getting into my cups. I looked down in my glass. Damnit, foiled by whiskey again. That was the problem with falling in love with it. When it was least expected, the drink folded in on itself and made you the bad guy.

Michael slammed down his glass and leaned forward to take mine from me. "You're cut off." He swiped my glass from me and set it down in front of himself.

"Nuh uh." I waved my hand. The bartender came over with another whiskey. Michael merely groaned.

"I made a deal." I smiled, feeling all smart with myself. "Ahem... You were saying?"

Michael glared at me. "I don't know if I can talk to you properly right now."

"Of course you can!" I realized I spoke too loudly, catching and shushing myself. My next words were more hushed. "You spent a lot of sexy time with another woman, then you killed her. Right?" I took a swig from my glass. "They cast a spell, sent me away, and I turned feral. Now we're in Norway, and we're going to beat those SpellCasters to a pulp. That about cover it?"

Michael's head fell forward, and he shook it in defeat. "Yes. That's about it."

"Good! Now what?"

"I need you to listen."

"I *am* listening!"

"What do we know about the SpellCasters? I mean, really know about them?"

"They're mean."

"Right, but more than that?"

"They're super attractive."

His head popped up. "C'mon, Celie. *Please* focus."

"Okay, okay." I put my glass down. Placing my hands up to my temples, I flattened my palms against them and thought really, really hard. "They have elemental powers?"

"Ah good!" Michael was pleased he was finally getting somewhere with me. I raised my glass, and he reluctantly clinked his to mine. "So, they have elemental powers. What are some ways we can combat that?"

I pulled back my arm, taking another swallow from my glass and draining it, feeling the cold ice against my lips. Placing the glass down on the table, I tilted my head to the side. "Maybe we could fight fire with fire?"

"How do you mean?"

"No no no... Not fire with fire. Um..." I stared at him for a minute and then felt a 'eureka' strike me. I opened my eyes wider and spoke in a whisper. "We can fight *fire* with *water*."

"Eh?" Michael raised a single eyebrow at me in confusion.

"Well, water hurts fire. And fire hurts air, right? They have these powers that use these things. So maybe we can use what they have...uh...against each other...?"

I thought Michael grinned at me, but he was a little blurry. Just in case, I gave him my best lopsided grin.

"Now we're getting somewhere. We fight fire with water, but how?" He leaned forward, his elbows on the table. He had rolled up the sleeves of his button-down shirt and left his muscular forearms exposed. I glanced down from his eyes for just a moment to look at his arms and swallowed; they were tantalizing.

"Um..."

"You with me?"

"Yeah, I..." I was lust-struck, so I stopped to shake my head. "I'm sorry, what were we talking about?"

Michael sighed in frustration. Just as I began to open my mouth, my new Samsung cell phone on the table began to ring. Caller ID showed it was Xander.

"Never mind. We'll talk about this later." He reached for my phone, then paused. "May I?"

I gestured for him to proceed. I figured I wasn't in the best condition to carry on a conversation anyway. He picked up the phone and answered it.

"Xander, hello... Okay, sure. Just a moment."

Michael stood up and gestured for me to follow him. We walked to the back of the bar area and sat down at another table far away from the customers near the bar itself. I looked at Michael, and he set the phone on the table, placing the call on speakerphone. He adjusted the volume to ensure we could hear it but the others up front could not.

"Okay, go ahead, Xander."

"Thanks, Mike. Hey, Celie."

I smiled. "Hey, buddy! How's things? You and Kat make it to Boston, okay?"

"We sure did. We've got Ricky here with us, too."

"Please tell everyone I said hi!" I said and waved at the phone. Michael watched me and laughed. I smirked; at least I was amusing when I was swacked.

"Will do. Now onto the news. Ricky pulled some more data."

"Did you find them?" asked Michael.

"Find who? Other vamps?" I queried, excited at the prospect of meeting more of my (new) kind. Michael held his finger to his lips, urging me to lower my voice. I pretended to lock my lips and throw away the key.

"Yes, but they aren't very trusting of us. Something about Ricky set them off."

"Really?" said Michael, confusion in his voice. He'd only met Ricky once and nothing had seemed odd about him. "That's interesting... Tell me more."

"We arrived in Boston yesterday morning; Ricky met us at the airport. We all checked into a hotel and immediately headed over to this restaurant off Beacon Street, one that Ricky had told us was a hangout for you guys. When we got there, it was pretty obvious (to me anyway) that vampires were there."

"How so?"

"There was...I don't know, something in the air? I can't explain it, except to say that my instincts were firing on all cylinders."

"Fair enough."

I 'unlocked' my mouth. "So what happened? Did they approach you?" I was intrigued and desperate to know more about the Boston vampires.

"They did. A black vampire named James approached me. He was curious what I was doing with a white girl and an Asian vampire."

I sat down in front of my phone, leaning forward to hear better. "What did he say?"

"He asked what we were doing there and gave the nastiest look to Ricky."

Michael and I exchanged glances. I spoke up first. "Maybe they thought Ricky was giving up secrets?"

"No. It was more than that. There was something going on there that no one would talk about."

Michael's brow furrowed, and he sat back in his chair, stroking his chin. "Hmm..." After a moment, he leaned forward again, but he was definitely perplexed. "So what happened after the introductions?"

"That's just it: nothing."

"Nothing?"

"Not a damn thing. After we introduced ourselves and explained that we were looking for more information on the SpellCasters, we were basically ostracized. You could physically *see* everyone move further away from us. I mean, shit, Michael—I haven't felt so fuckin' segregated since that time I lived in the Midwest back in '92."

"Well, at least we know we're onto something." Michael looked up from the phone to me. "They're clearly afraid."

"Hell of a lot of good that does us."

Michael smirked. "It tells us that they know about the SpellCasters. Perhaps one of them knows more than they're letting on?"

I smirked back. "Good luck getting it out of them. If they reacted this way on introduction, how are we supposed to get anything extra from them? I doubt they'll give us any intel voluntarily."

Xander piped up. "I think I've got an idea to help with that."

"Oh? Do tell."

"I think we should send Ricky back alone." Michael and I looked at each other again, unsure what to say. Before we could say anything, Xander continued. "Kat and I already asked him to go, and he said yes. He's going to head over there this evening, to see what he can learn."

"Can we fit him with a wire or something?" I'd seen it in the movies and on television, so it had to work, right?

Michael looked at me, incredulous that I would ask something so asinine. "A wire? This isn't 1975, Celie. The other vampires would hear its electronic hum. You *know* that."

"I know that, silly. I'm just sayin', if we could listen in, maybe we could get a better understanding of why he's setting them off?"

"It's not a bad idea." Xander was clearly on my side.

Michael gave the phone an eyeful, then looked back up at me. "No way. The vampires would never let anyone, let alone another of their own kind, inside a place like that wearing a wire; they're too noisy. Whoever was wearing it would be thrown out at best, maimed at worst. It's a bad idea."

"What if it wasn't a wire?"

Now Xander had piqued my interest. "Such as?"

"There are mini voice-activated recording devices. No bigger than a pencil tip. We could fit one of those on Ricky. It could transmit to us back at the hotel."

"That sounds perfect!"

Michael, however, didn't look so enthusiastic. "You're sure this thing would be quiet? I mean, so quiet as to border on *silent.*"

"Yes, this thing only records when it hears voices, and those voices can be up 45 feet away. It'll do the job without putting off a sound."

"Okay." It was crystal clear Michael was still reluctant. "Let's put this in motion, but I want Ricky to be on his guard. If anything goes sideways, I want him out of there."

"Roger that."

"How's Kat doing?" I asked.

"She's good. Hang on, I'll put her on."

After a moment, I heard my girl come on the line. "Hiya!"

"Hi, Kat" I smiled automatically. "How are you? I'm so glad you two are safe."

"Us, too. When Xander told me we had to go, that the SpellCasters were coming, I was pretty freaked out. Fortunately, we made it to the airport super-fast."

"That's so good. Yeah, I called him as soon as I found out."

"Thank you for that. Are you two okay?"

"Yup! We're in–" I paused and looked at Michael, who shook his head. "—another country that I can't tell you about...?"

"What? What do you mean you can't tell me?" Confusion laced every word.

"It's probably best that you don't know exactly where we are—at least, not yet."

"Why? Do you think we're a leak?"

"No! No, nothing like that. We're just trying to limit the number of ways the SpellCasters might be able to figure out where we're located."

"And you think we're going to tell them? What the fuck, Celie?"

"No, Kat. Just—no. The idea is that if you get captured by them, the less you know, the better."

"I'd never tell them anything. Not a single goddamned thing."

"I know, sweetie, but we don't know the extent of their powers. What if they have a way they could force you to tell them? Like some sort of mind-control? You might tell them involuntarily."

Kat huffed audibly, but I could tell she knew I was right. "Fine. *Fine*. Keep your secrets."

"I'm sorry, Kat. You know I'd tell you if I could, but–"

I heard some shuffling, and the next thing I knew, Xander was back on the phone. Kat was angry, but I knew that deep down she understood. Hearing that your friend has to keep things from you feels like a betrayal of trust, so she was justified in her hurt feelings. It was going to take some time for her to come around to our way of thinking and release her anger. I only hoped it would be sooner rather than later.

Michael and Xander talked more about the plan to send Ricky back in with the recording device. Once they had the details synced up, they agreed to talk again later in another 24 hours. Xander hung up on his side and Michael turned to me. His expression was a little accusatory.

"Calm your tits; I'm sober again."

Michael chuckled and handed my phone over to me. "Now we wait."

"Any thoughts on what would have them so standoffish about Ricky?"

"I've been wondering about that myself." Michael glanced past me to make sure no one had gotten closer to us. He re-engaged eye contact with me before he spoke. "How long have you known Ricky? I mean, when did you meet him?"

"Oh, um... I think Kat introduced me to him about ten years ago?"

"Where does she know him from?"

"College, she said. They had some class together... I think it was English Lit? I honestly can't remember..."

"That's okay. Good. He's not someone new or who was following us."

"You can't think..."

"No—I mean, not necessarily—but I do think that having learned he's also a vampire, it's interesting that none of us had any inclination to even guess he was one."

"Well, I didn't hang out with him very much. However, looking back at things, I probably should have been paying closer attention." I leaned back in my chair. "Can I get a drink again? I think I need another one..."

Michael leaned back in his own chair. "Later. Tell me more about Ricky."

I sighed. "Okay, I'll tell you what I know."

I proceeded to relive experiences that I'd had with Ricky (and typically Kat, too) over the years, careful to keep the details impartial. We dove into my memories and discussed Ricky at length: his likes, his dislikes, times we spent together, etc. I struggled to find a time when Ricky hadn't been the life of the party or ready to lend a helping hand. It wasn't long before we both realized we needed to hear the conversation between Ricky and the Boston colony to really get to the bottom of things.

Now we had to wait.

Chapter Fourteen

The Boston Colony

Kat and Xander were on edge. Ricky was going to meet with the Boston colony members at the restaurant on Beacon Street. Not just that, but during his meeting, they could learn something about him that they didn't know before: something new, something dangerous... The prospects were daunting, and they were both anxious about what they would uncover.

Kat was especially nervous; afterall, she had introduced Ricky to her friends and her family. After meeting him in English Lit, they had become campus buddies and started hanging out after class, meeting for drinks or to see movies with friends. They shared laughs and secrets with each other. It had always seemed like Ricky was just a young, normal boy. It never occurred to her that he could be hiding a secret as big as being a vampire. That had quite literally blown her away, causing her to faint dead away and fall on her ass back at the hotel in Ireland.

Now she was watching Xander prep Ricky with a mini voice-recording device. Xander was fixing the device into Ricky's red jacket collar and showing him how it works. It was as small as a thumbtack but much sleeker and slate colored. If it was truly capable, it would record the entire conversation he was set to have with James the vampire, as well as any other vampires he encountered at the restaurant. The device would also transmit back to the hotel through a speaker, where she and Xander would be listening in on everything.

Kat wrung her hands like a desperate Victorian woman—she couldn't help herself. She was feeling horrible after her spat with Celie yesterday. Apologies were definitely in order. She was also a wreck over the SpellCasters having been so close to them back in Ireland. The fact that they barely escaped hadn't left her mind. Now this bit with Ricky left her borderline spastic, ready to fly off the handle, and she was afraid she would say something out of fear that would set things off.

Reining herself in, Kat watched Xander finish prepping Ricky with the recorder. He turned to her and nodded, and she gave him her most winning smile. He looked back at Ricky and gave him a pat on the back.

Xander was the only bright spot in this entire fiasco. It was his courage, his strength, and his cool head that kept her from going over the edge. His experience in the military and with the government had given him insight into these kinds of events, ones that involved dastardly villains and enormous odds. The warmth, love, and patience he had shown her since the SpellCasters had arrived was enough to make her fall in love with him all over again, every single day.

She had Celie to thank for their introduction. Ever since she met him, she felt like a part of herself was no longer hollow, that he had somehow completed part of her. She knew he felt it, too: the way he looked at her, the way he touched her, the way he said her name... Every bit of what they had was magical, and she was more than in love with her magician.

Right now, with Ricky about to head out the door, Kat wanted to say something to him, but what? What could she say to make things better? 'Watch your back'? 'Stay safe'? 'Keep a cool head and don't blow this, Ricky'? It all seemed terribly cliché and ridiculous. He was a vampire, capable of abilities they didn't know and probably couldn't even fathom. There was also the chance he was responsible for some really bad shit in their lives if they weren't careful. Nothing she could think of seemed sufficient. So when the time came that Ricky was heading out, she said the only three words to him that came to mind in that moment.

"Hey Ricky?"

"Yeah, Katie-kat?"

"Break a leg."

Ricky laughed. "Not if I can help it, kid." Then he was gone, the door closing behind him quietly—slowly—as if it was also saying good-bye.

The silence in the room was deafening. Kat stared at the door for a minute, unsure if they had made the right decision. Could they trust Ricky? Really trust him? What if he sided with the colony over them and came back to the hotel to rip them to pieces? What if Ricky was a bad guy, and the colony killed him before coming back to finish them off? What if Ricky just bailed, and they were left with nothing? The latter was the best negative option, but it would still hurt if it came true.

Turning around, Kat looked at Xander, sure that her fear was showing.

"Now that's no good, Kat." Xander walked over to her and took her hands in his. Kat loved how large his hands were, making her own feel small and tiny. She lowered her head and refused to look up at him.

"I'm sorry. I just keep thinking the worst is going to happen."

Xander put a finger under her chin and lifted her head until she was looking up at him. He stood nearly eight inches taller than her, so she had to raise it quite a bit. Once she did, she was looking into his stunning golden eyes and immediately sighed. He was so incredibly gorgeous.

"I know you are. Let's remember that we can hear everything that'll be going on in there. We'll know if something is up, and if that happens, we'll leave. It's as simple as that."

"But what if–"

"No 'what ifs' today. We're going to put our trust in Ricky that this will all work out."

Kat looked away. She felt tears welling up in her eyes and didn't want him to see them.

Too late, Xander saw how afraid she was, and he pulled her in close. Placing a kiss on her forehead, he then placed one on her left eye, followed by one on her right. She melted into him as he leaned lower still to place a kiss on her lips, and she relished feeling the softness and fullness of him as he tasted her.

Before long, they were eagerly stripping each other of their clothes.

Kat ran her hands over Xander's bare ebony skin, feeling her anxiety flee as she was overtaken by the desire to be taken in the bedroom. As Xander reached behind her to undo her bra, she leaned forward and whispered to him—hot, intense, erotic nothings in his ear. He immediately stopped what he was doing and bent down to scoop her up into his arms. Carrying her into the bedroom, he stopped just at the bed's edge and put Kat down, spinning her around and bending her over. He leaned down, pulling her panties down past her hips, and placing a love bite on her backside. She yelped and giggled.

Xander was already hard as a rock for her. He knelt down and found the softest parts of Kat, then began nuzzling and licking her clit. Tasting her was like tasting candy, and he had a sweet tooth. He suckled at her and made her softly moan as he slid one finger after another inside of her. Once he felt her clench around him, he knew she was ready. He stood up and, taking his large cock in his hand, slid inside her from behind. Kat's heavy moan nearly undid him as he began to thrust into her, over and over, feeling himself growing harder, her sheath tighter.

"C'mon baby, come for me." He was eager to feel her pulsate around him. He saw her slip a hand underneath herself, her breathing growing erratic within moments. He continued to thrust, squeezing her backside, then slowing down to slip deeper and deeper into her beautiful pink flesh.

Then he felt it, the gentle squeeze from within, a quake that seemed to be all around him, growing tighter and tighter until she clenched down on him, surrounding him hard with her tight heat. He thrust faster now, urged on by her orgasm until he exploded, pouring himself into her and calling her name. He braced himself with a hand on her lower back, another holding her hip, as the sensations rocked them both.

After a few moments, they were both finished completely, the storm having settled. Xander slowly slipped out, and Kat crawled forward and rolled over. He moved onto the bed after her and lay beside her. He kissed her, long and slow, telling her how much he loved her and caressing her arm. Kat told him she loved him, too, stroking his chest gently with her left hand and wrapping her left leg around his hip to keep him close. They lay like that for a time, close and quiet.

When the speaker picked up Ricky's voice, they were forced to rejoin reality.

Ricky was walking down Beacon Street, heading towards the restaurant, and he looked totally relaxed. There was something almost robotic about him. He seemed to not have a care in the world, which was surprising considering he was about to walk into the lion's den. Yet, Ricky was at ease, moving smoothly and calmly, even smiling.

He had serious intentions, and nothing was going to deter him from getting what he wanted.

Upon arrival at the designated spot, he walked up to the front door and opened it, feeling the whoosh of stale air from inside slap him across the face. He stepped inside and the door closed angrily behind him, slamming shut. He turned around, and James the vampire was standing there, his hand still on the door. Ricky smiled at him, but James would have none of it. Without taking his eyes off of Ricky, James' hulking frame walked around him, giving him a wide berth, and gesturing for Ricky to follow him to the back stairs. When they reached the stairs, James had Ricky go first, heading down into the basement below.

A sickly white light tinged with green lit the bottom of the stairs where a door waited for Ricky, wooden and closed. He stopped in front of it, and upon reaching the bottom of the staircase, James reached around Ricky and opened the door, signaling that Ricky should go inside. Without missing a beat, Ricky stepped through the doorway.

The colony was waiting for him; vampires of every gender, age, height, and ethnicity standing about the room. They had been talking amongst themselves, but all turned to examine him once he entered. It was this moment that caused Ricky to experience apprehension. There were so many of them...

Could he get away with this?

Kat and Xander hovered over the speaker, listening dutifully as voices were hushed. After a moment, a singular one came through the speaker, one of authority. It was a woman's voice, and she sounded strong, regal, and most definitely angry.

"How *dare* you defile our home this way, Ricky Yun! Bringing those normals into our sanctuary... We should rip your limbs from you." Each word was laced with contempt.

"My apologies, Haven Mother. I only did what was needed."

"What was needed? What was needed! You *merely* violated one of our most sacred laws: to never bring normals into a vampire sanctuary. You *know* this!"

Kat and Xander exchanged nervous glances with each other. The Haven Mother was most certainly the leader of the colony, and by her tone, it sounded like Ricky was in some serious trouble. They hoped he could talk his way out of it.

"You are right, Haven Mother. I deserve punishment. However, these normals are my friends, and we need your assistance against the SpellCasters."

A gasp rose from the other vampires; he had touched a nerve.

"The SpellCasters?" Murmurs were growing louder throughout the space. "Silence!" she shouted, and the voices died down. "You say the SpellCasters are seeking you?"

"Not me. Michael Hawkins and Cecelia Moore."

"They are not part of this coven." There was grave finality in her statement.

"I know this. Neither am I, but you gave me refuge here once."

"We did. Are we to regret that now?"

"No, Haven Mother." He paused for a moment before getting to the point. "We're seeking knowledge that may help us defend them against the SpellCasters."

Silence poured through the speaker like loud static.

"Please."

More silence.

"We are desperate." The distress in his voice was convincing enough for Kat and Xander to believe him. Kat's fears about Ricky's intentions eased a little.

There was a loud, heavy sigh. "Why should we assist you, young one?"

"It is our hope that we can discover a way to beat them. We can pass this knowledge on to all of you."

"You—" she scoffed, "—you think we haven't examined the text? Impudent child. We have all the knowledge held within these walls, as well as some that isn't."

"I meant no disrespect, Haven Mother. We are merely seeking salvation."

Another round of silence came through the speaker. It lasted a few seconds before the Haven Mother spoke again. "I don't believe you will learn anything new. However, you may borrow our text. Bring it back within 24 hours but hold it no longer! Return it to us, or we *will* hunt you down and cleave your flesh."

"Yes, Haven Mother."

The voices from the colony members resumed in earnest. Ricky said nothing further except a 'thank you' here and there. Steps were heard and some rustling, as if through papers. After another fifteen minutes, silence had overtaken the speaker; they presumed Ricky had left the premises.

Xander looked over at Kat, who was biting her nails. He reached out and grabbed her hand. She looked pensive and troubled, which he was positive was exactly how he looked, too.

"Say something."

"Like what?"

"That was good news from the colony. They have writings about the SpellCasters. We'll be able to give Mike and Celie more information to fight them."

"That's true."

"So, what's eating you up?"

"I'm not sure? It's like... Ugh..." she groaned in frustration. "It's like I feel like there's something we don't know..."

"Such as?"

"It's just...I don't know, a feeling, maybe?" Her fingertips continued to fidget despite Xander holding her hand.

"Okay then. Say that what you're feeling is correct, that something else is going on—any guesses as to what it is?"

Kat inhaled, held her breath for a moment, then looked right in Xander's eyes and blurted out, "I think Ricky is pulling some shit behind our back."

"What? Like he's gonna betray us?"

"Yeah. Exactly."

Shocked, Xander stood there, staring into Kat's eyes, his own wide with surprise. He had expected her to say a lot of things, but not that. *She* was the one who introduced them all to Ricky. *She* was the one who had known him for years and years. They were friends since college, and she'd even brought Ricky into her home—her *home*. Why would she think he would betray them?

Kat turned away from Xander, forcing him to release her hand as she took a few steps and began pacing the room. Her breathing was quick, borderline hyperventilating. She was stressed and began rambling all of her logic out loud.

"For starters, he's been quiet—and kinda strange. I can't explain it. I've known him for such a long time, you know?" She eyed Xander, who simply nodded, then she refocused her pacing. "Ever since we contacted him—you know, to help us find Celie—I got this strange vibe from him, like he was being secretive, right? He sounded serious with them, while we were listening just now, and maybe it's nothing—maybe that was just from his history with them? I can't explain it, Xander. I just get this creepy feeling, like in the pit of my stomach? I know this doesn't make sense, and I wish I could make it *make sense*. He's just been so weird, and now I'm worried I'm right. I'm worried that he is going to pull a fast one on us and somehow rat us out to the vampires or SpellCasters—or maybe something even *worse*. He's getting this important information—this really, *really* important information—and what...what if he doesn't give it to us? What if he just takes off with it? What if this was all a ruse, and he's been playing us this whole time? I just don't know, and I *hate* not knowing, you know?"

Kat continued to pace, and the phone rang. Keeping an eye on Kat as she paced and vocalized her thoughts to an audience of one, Xander reached across the table and picked up his cell phone. It was Celie.

"Hey, Celie."

"Hi, Xander. Any news?"

"Not exactly. We're waiting for Ricky to get back from the meeting."

"Were you able to listen in on the conversation with the colony?"

"Yeah. He's getting some sort of text from them? I don't know; it's something they have written about the SpellCasters."

"That's fantastic!"

"It *is* fantastic, but..."

"But what?" asked Michael. Xander realized he was on speakerphone at that point.

"Hey Mike. How are you?"

"I'm fine. What were you going to say?"

Xander ran his palm from the top of his head down his face. "Kat is..." He sighed. "We're having some doubts and concerns over here." He continued to watch Kat moving back and forth.

"Doubts? About what?"

"About Ricky."

"Why?"

"Is that Kat back there?" The sound of Kat's incessant talking was concerning Celie.

"Yeah, she's been going on and on for a hot minute."

"What's going on?" When he hesitated to respond, Celie pushed. "Seriously, Xander—tell me what's going on."

"Kat's...Kat's got a gut feeling that Ricky is gonna betray us."

"For real? Why?"

"For real. She's not sure; it's just a feeling, but that's why we're waiting it out."

Michael's voice was stern and low—menacing, even. "How long has it been since he left the restaurant?"

"About ten minutes, give or take."

"And how long did it take for him to get there?"

"About thirty."

"So, we have twenty minutes until he arrives back at the hotel?"

"That's right."

"Fine. We'll wait. We give him the time to show, and if he doesn't, we'll go find *him*."

And wait they did. For 45 long minutes, they waited, with Kat pacing and Xander monitoring the exteriors. For 45 agonizing minutes, they stared at the hotel room door, expecting it to open—hoping Ricky would come walking through with a smartass remark and the vampire text.

But after 45 minutes, nothing had happened. No one opened the hotel room door. Ricky never showed, Kat cried, and Xander fumed. On the speakerphone, Michael growled, and Celie cursed. They all had their answer.

Ricky had betrayed them.

Chapter Fifteen

Narrow Escape

Ricky had escaped. No, not just escaped: that rat bastard had stolen the vampire text about the SpellCasters right out from under them.

I couldn't believe it. After knowing this kid for all these years, to learn that he could just up and betray us was mind-blowing. I thought I felt my brain implode. Michael was *pissed* and incredibly riled up at the young vampire for what he had done to us. Now we had even less information than before.

I watched Michael fume and seethe. He was standing on the balcony of our hotel room, staring out across the fjord. His jaw was clenched, and his muscles rippled with angry tension. His arms were folded in front of his chest, rising and falling as he breathed. He made no sound. When I stepped forward and placed a hand on his shoulder, he turned to me, and the rage was there in his eyes, cold and immovable.

If we ever found Ricky, Michael would rip him apart.

"Hey, we'll figure this out." I wanted to soften him some. I was angry, too, but there was an intensity to Michael's anger that I simply couldn't bear. I felt the need to diffuse him.

The cold in his eyes thawed just a little. Unfolding his arms, Michael reached over and placed a hand to my cheek. I leaned into his palm, hoping he could see the concern in my eyes. He did, giving me a small smile, and it was just enough to know that he wouldn't stay this angry around me for long. A moment later, his hand dropped back to his side, and he turned back to the view, ice returning to his gaze.

I sighed. Turning around, I began to pack up our things. We had been in Geiranger, Norway for two days, and that was two days too long. Who knew when the SpellCasters might show up for us? Considering our short time there, we had very little to pack—some clothes, my phone—but I wanted any evidence of us to be gone. I proceeded to place them in souvenir bags that we had obtained from one of the local gift shops along with a trinket I had grabbed.

Then I felt it, almost like a vibration pulsating lightly through the air. I heard Michael inhale sharply, and he growled, deep and strong. Turning, I saw his hands braced against the doorframe of the balcony. He stared out the glass, the wood splintering beneath his tight grip. I rushed over to the window, anxious to see what had provoked him. As I took the handful of steps to meet him, I prayed it wasn't what I thought, prayed we had more time.

I was wrong.

The SpellCasters were here, on the hotel grounds. The three of them had followed us from Ireland and were approaching the hotel, walking next to each other as if marching toward battle. The one in the middle, a tall woman with bright red hair and long legs, looked up and saw us. She reached out on either side of herself, stopping them in their tracks, and pointed up. A smile crept onto her face, and I felt myself go cold: it was an evil, malignant smile full of diabolical promise.

Suddenly they were rushing forward into the hotel. I screamed, startled by how fast they moved. Michael swung around. Grabbing my phone from the bed and pulling me close, he took me in his arms and ported us out of there.

I felt the vacuum of space—of time. Darkness swallowed me whole, with winds howling around me. I could still feel Michael's body against mine, but he was like a jet-black shape that wrapped itself in shadows and smoke around my body. I closed my eyes, biding my time until the transport was over. It didn't take long for light to breakthrough my eyelids, an orange glow permeating my vision. I opened my eyes, and we were back home.

Home.

Michael had ported us to just outside our home in Bantum, at the bottom of the steps outside the front door, the fountain behind him. I stepped back from Michael's arms, inhaling the cool air and smiling. I spun around, my arms outstretched, feeling overjoyed to be back where we were meant to be. After a moment of spinning, I brought myself to a stop, turning around to see Michael. He was watching me with a wide grin on his face.

"Thank you for bringing us home." Then I went to him, placed my hands on either side of his face, and planted a passionate kiss on his lips. He put his hands on my shoulders and pulled me in close. I kissed him for only a minute or two before letting go. I didn't want to release him, but I had to.

We had work to do.

We both headed up the steps and inside. Entering the main hall, I looked around, having been away from home for weeks. My brow furrowed; something was different.

"Where are my things?" Michael had moved past me to head into the library. I called out to him. "I don't see any of my stuff here...?"

Exercising extreme caution, Michael slowly came around the corner at the far end of the hallway. "Don't be alarmed, but they took everything."

"They *what*? Why? Why would they need my things?" I turned to the hall table gesturing to an empty space. "Like, why on earth would they need my elephant statue? What would be the point of taking *that*?"

Michael cleared his throat. "It was apparently part of the spell they cast on me—the one to make me forget you. They...they removed anything that would remind me of you."

I felt my vision grow dark, and I began to see red, but this time it was in rage: I was furious. "Those bastards." I felt my fangs begin to grow. "I'm going to shred them to pieces—little, tiny fucking pieces."

Michael walked over to me and took me by my shoulders. "While your anger is justified, please save it for the real fight ahead."

I felt him sort of 'boop' my mind, and I shook my head as if I was clearing out the rage. My eyes met his. "You really didn't remember me?"

I could hear the sadness in my own voice. I wished I could hide it, but I wasn't built to hide my emotions well. Wearing masks wasn't really my thing. I was a lifetime member of the 'Wear your Heart on your Sleeve' club.

His brow furrowed, and then he suddenly smiled. "Actually, there were times I *did* remember you—I just didn't know it at the time. There were bits and pieces of you here that wouldn't let me go." He took my hand and kissed the inside of my wrist. "Even if their spells made my mind forget, my heart never let you go."

"Really?" The romantic part of me began swooning for him all over again.

"Yes, love. I saw you here, in our home. I didn't know who you were, but I knew that I loved you." He held my hand to the side of his face and sighed. "You know you hold my heart in your hands, don't you?"

"Aww…" That did it. I swooned and pulled him toward me, kissing him so I could taste him and breathe him in. He caught me and kissed me back, our lips saying everything we couldn't in that moment.

I broke the kiss first. "Someday, this will all be behind us. But right now, just know that I love you, Mike. So much."

"I'll always love you, Celie." He took my hand again and entwined our fingers. "Now, let's get ready. We need to prepare ourselves against the SpellCasters. They'll be coming for us again, and we need to be ready."

"I can't believe how quickly they found us."

"I can. They have various spells and means of locating things, including people. We can't take it lightly."

"We can't stay here, then?" I pouted, disappointed we would have to leave home again.

"No, I don't think so. We also have some places we need to go, and we need to track down Ricky and find that text."

"Ooh, when I find that bag of dicks, I'm going to scratch his eyes out."

"Before you do, let me tackle him. We don't know his abilities, and I'd prefer to test them out on myself rather than you."

"But I—"

"Please don't argue with me on this."

I acquiesced and nodded in agreement. My abilities were still too new, and we didn't know how old Ricky was. Unfortunately, Michael was right.

With that, I stuck my hand out and Michael handed me my phone so I could call Kat. Hopefully she wasn't still mad at me. I hated when we were arguing with each other. Since she was like a sister to me, the world just didn't feel right when I couldn't call her or talk with her.

I pressed the 'on' button and my Samsung came alive. Better still, it showed 14 missed calls from Kat. I sighed in relief. Tapping my phone,

I dialed her cell phone number. I would swear she answered it before it really had a chance to ring.

"Hello?"

"There you are. Hi Kat."

"Celie? Good god, woman! Where have you been? Are you okay? I tried calling you a thousand times!"

"I saw that. I'm sorry! We had a little...kerfuffle."

"What happened?"

"SpellCasters showed up."

"Are you fucking serious? They were there?"

"Yes. We saw them walking up the hillside toward our hotel, so Mike grabbed me and ported us out of there."

"That's a handy thing to have—that porting business. I'm sure it beats flying, anyway."

"Right now, absolutely." I paused, softening my tone. "Hey, are you still mad at me? I know you were just concerned, and I'm sorry that I couldn't–"

"That's over and done with, sweetie. I can't stay mad at you!"

"Oh, thank god. I was so worried!"

"Don't be. I can be a stubborn ass. Can you tell me where you were hiding, though? I'm super curious!"

"Norway."

"Norway? Really? Isn't that place really cold?"

"It was chilly where we were, but Mike kept me warm."

"Ha ha ha, I bet!" laughed Kat, and it was so amazing to hear considering our situation.

"On that note, I need your help again."

"Sure. Whatcha got?"

"We're back in the US, and–"

"Yay!"

"–we want to track down Ricky to get the SpellCaster text from him. Any thoughts on where he might have gone?"

"Hmm... Typically he was at home? He lives just outside Bantum, you know, in one of those brownstones off Richmond Avenue."

"Oh really? I know where those are!"

"Mmm hmm! I'll text you his address."

"Please do it fast. We're not sure how much longer we can stay where we are. The SpellCasters could be right on our heels."

"Understood. Texting...gimme a sec...there! You should have it." I felt my phone vibrate at my ear.

"Thanks!"

"Don't mention it."

"Okay, I've gotta go. I'll call you later after we've hit up his address and had a little 'conversation' with him."

"Ooh, yes. Please do." Kat had a devilish lilt in her voice.

"Ciao, babe."

"Ciao."

I hung up and turned to Michael. "We've got his address."

A wicked smile crept across his face. "Let's go."

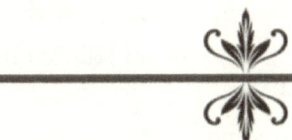

We rolled up outside Ricky's address in Michael's car, the vehicle clock telling us it was close to midnight. I climbed out of the passenger side, feeling my palms sweating and wiped them on my pant legs. I stepped up onto the curb, my right hand on top of the car door frame, and I looked over at Michael standing on the driver's side. He winked at me, and I felt slightly better.

Knowing he was with me was reassuring, as I wasn't sure I could do this by myself. It had been a while since I had to fight anyone, and that was different. I hated that demon. Ricky was a friend, or he had been before he took the SpellCaster text.

Why did he do it? Did he hate us? Were we merely a means to an end? I needed to find out, needed to get some answers.

Michael and I shut our respective doors, met on the sidewalk, and proceeded up the brownstone steps to Ricky's front door. In front of the black front door, I extended my hand but paused before knocking. I looked at Michael, and he nodded. Turning back to the door, I rapped three times and stepped back, waiting for someone to answer.

We didn't have to wait long.

Wearing a gray hoodie and black athletic pants, Ricky peeked out the window. As soon as he saw us, he bolted. Michael reached back and threw a punch at the door, slamming it inward and knocking it off the hinges. I followed him as he walked inside, hearing the remains of the doorway crunch under his black boots.

Inside, Ricky had run up the stairs to the second floor. Michael stared up the flight and growled, then he disappeared. I stood at the bottom of the stairs and listened, hearing crashes and banging coming from above. There were snarls and roars, and sometimes the sounds jumped from the front of the brownstone to the back. After a few minutes, the sounds quieted, and I stood still, willing my ears to hear anything from upstairs. Nothing.

All of a sudden, Michael appeared in the room, holding a bloody and beaten Ricky by his hood. Ricky was tugging at his hold a little, but it was clear he didn't have any fight left in him. I stepped forward and raised Ricky's head by his chin, so he could look me in the eye while Michael held onto him.

"Why, Ricky? Why did you take it?"

Eyes closed, Ricky squirmed again and then stopped. He opened his eyes, and his pupils were slitted.

He was shifting, transforming, and becoming something new.

His limbs shrank up into his clothes, sleeves and pant legs growing slack. His face elongated, chin and mouth spreading wide and outward. Hair fell out of his head to the floor, and a forked tongue darted out of his mouth. Skin split into scales and took on a metallic sheen. The entire process only took a matter of seconds, and once it was complete, a giant snake was now in Ricky's place. Michael was holding the hoodie with nothing in it, watching as the snake piled up on the floor at our feet and began to slither away.

"Grab it!" I squealed, unable to get past my fear of snakes. I felt like an elephant with a mouse. It didn't matter that I could become a panther—snakes were off limits.

Michael released the clothing and dove after the snake, but it moved faster than he anticipated. The slick, scaly exterior and sinewy body made it hard for him to grasp. Before Michael could get a hold of him, Ricky had slithered out the back, pushing past a screen door, and sliding down a drainage hole into the sewage system. Just missing the tail, Michael stopped at the pipe opening and shouted into it, roaring in frustration.

From inside the house, I called out to Michael to come in. I watched him push himself up into a standing position, dusting himself off. Turning, he walked back to the house and opened the screen door, a loud 'whack' sound reaching my ears when he released it. Walking towards me, I could see the defeat on his face. He looked down at his shoes, both frustrated and a touch embarrassed.

"Don't worry, we'll find him."

"I know." He scanned the room. "Until then, let's check the house for the text. I doubt he took it with him."

I laughed. "Of course. I'll take upstairs."

I ran over to the stairs and headed up, taking the steps two at a time. Once I reached the top, I started searching the room to my left. I rifled through papers, overturned bedding, and tore into the contents of his dresser. Nothing. Exiting that room, I went to the next and repeated my steps. I could hear Michael downstairs ripping each room apart. Based on the sounds, he was taking his frustration out on the furniture.

It wasn't until I reached the third room that I found the text. Lying atop a cheap folding table was an ancient book, bound in olive green leather, covered in dust, and emblazoned with strange symbols in gold leaf foil. I lifted the book from the table, and all of a sudden, I felt spooked by the mysteries held inside. No strange wind swept through the room, and no mysterious voices began chanting. However, the weight of the book's knowledge contained felt powerful.

I have it. I stared down at the book, running my right hand over the cover.

Great. Let's get back to the house.

I'll be right there. This thing is heavy, in more ways than one.

I'll be waiting in the car.

While I stood there in Ricky's room, and for no reason other than curiosity, I opened the book. The pages were fine parchment, inscribed with black ink, and covered in script and symbols. They were discolored and smelled as if the book had been created centuries ago; I could only guess at what we would learn. Each page in the book bore incredible detail after detail about the SpellCasters throughout the years: historical facts, spells, the vampire hunts, etc. Thumbing through the book, I stumbled across one that discussed the origins of the SpellCasters.

Best to review that with Mike.

Then a particular entry caught my eye. It talked about how vampires were chosen by the SpellCasters for hunting, and it sent a chill down my spine:

"A call is placed by one so bold with the intent to engage the SpellCasters for delivering judgement. That person or group would pay the price in blood. They testify to the vampire's dealings and whereabouts, after which all talk ceases until the judgement has been rendered. Anyone may call upon the SpellCasters for this purpose including other vampires."

That's when the revelation dawned on me. I slammed the book shut and raced down the stairs. Running out the front door, I didn't even bother to close it behind me. I made my way down the front steps and came close to hitting the side of the car, I ran up to it so fast. Grabbing the door handle, I jerked the door open and jumped in, letting the car door slam hard behind me. Michael looked over at me, startled at my exuberance. I barely caught my breath before blurting out the news.

"It was Ricky."

Michael looked at me, ready to ask me what I was talking about, when the realization hit him, too. "Are you absolutely sure?"

"Yes."

Michael snarled and punched the steering wheel. After a moment, he started up the car and took off from our space along the curb. He drove fast, almost too fast, but I understood and chose to hang on rather than say anything. I looked out the passenger window at the buildings and trees passing us by. I focused on the roar of the engine and the feel of the leather seat beneath me, anything to distract me from the truth...

Ricky had sent the SpellCasters.

Ionsáiteán

Ready, Set, Go

"They've made it home."

The three SpellCasters were on the lawn just behind Grønn Utsikt Hotel, out of sight of the many visitors and tourists. Brigit was pacing, her hefty boots digging into the dirt, while Rusalka danced across the grass like a fairy princess. Pavan was scrying again, bent over a map. The pendulum had ceased moving and was holding steady directly over Bantum. At his words, the female SpellCasters had stopped, giving him their full attention.

"Good, let's go get the bloodsuckers." Brigit pounded her fist into her palm, ready to get violent.

"Yes, let's get them!" Rusalka jumped up and down, her delicate feet bouncing in the grass.

"*Viraam.*" (Stop.) Pavan waved his hand at them and stood up straight. He was still angry that they had again lost their prey. This was the second time, and he would see to it that a third didn't happen.

"We need to handle this differently. We thought we had them locked down in Ireland, and they escaped. Now they have escaped us in Norway. Do you want to see it happen all over again?"

Pavan stared at Brigit, then Rusalka, who immediately ceased her bouncing. Each of them shook their heads. Truth be told, they were all growing tired of chasing after these *pishaach*. Normally a hunt was easier than this. Challenges were fun and all, but enough of that; the SpellCasters had a job to do. They were each ready to fulfill their obligation to the one who called them.

"Excellent. We need to anticipate their moves. They are at home, but they have this ability to...'jump' from location to location. I need you to put a stop to that." He pointed at Brigit.

"Of course."

"Rusalka?"

"Yes?" Rusalka eyeballed him with hopeful curiosity.

"Your job will be to warp their emotions."

"Perfect!"

Pavan addressed them both. "We'll need to travel back there. No, we will *not* be taking a commercial airline this time." Rusalka made a face and stuck out her tongue. He looked directly at Brigit. "I need you to transport us there." She nodded.

Pavan turned his attention back to the map, staring at the dot that represented Bantum. The image bore into his brain like a worm into an apple. He felt a storm raging within him.

In all the years he had been a SpellCaster, he had never encountered this much difficulty in capturing his quarry. Many centuries ago, he had been a djinn (commonly referred to a genie), granting thousands upon thousands of wishes, albeit deadly ones. He had trampled peasants and kings, given warlords their due, and taken empresses down from their lofty pedestals. Yet he was always thrown back into his prison, trapped inside a small bottle until the next victim came calling. It wasn't until the SpellCaster league had freed him from his cell that he turned his gifts into dedicated abilities, manipulating air and all its associated powers to hunt down vampires.

Pavan heaved a heavy sigh. He missed Meyana's sensibility. If only they had listened to her when she wanted to collapse the vampire home into a sinkhole. That would have done the trick.

Yes, they would annihilate the vampires this time around. Third time's the charm, yes?

Chapter Sixteen

Origins

"No. Just no. That's not possible."

"It is, Kat. Ricky is the one who called the SpellCasters and sent them after us." Warily, I watched the news sink in. As soon as it hit her, her face turned into the visage of rage.

"I'll murder him. Snake or no snake, he's dead. I can't *believe* I fell for his act! What a lowdown, dirty vampire!" She stopped and turned to me. "Sorry."

"No offense taken. I get it. You're angry. We all are. Now we need to regroup and figure out how to tackle the SpellCasters and him. Who knows what crap they have up their magical sleeves..."

"Luckily you guys found the book. That'll help."

"We hope so."

"Well, let's get crackin'! Let's open up this damn thing and get to work!"

I nodded, and Michael dropped the text onto the table. Without hesitation, we began to pour over the text laid out before us.

After Michael and I had left Ricky's brownstone, it occurred to us that we couldn't go back home. Not yet anyway. That would be the first place the SpellCasters would surely look for us. We had to keep moving. Traveling along the interior, we took as many backroads as we could to get to Xander and Kat on the outskirts of Boston. We secured a room in a nearby hotel and then met them at theirs.

Now we stood around the oak table in their room, examining a centuries-old text about the beings that were sent to kill us.

It was amazing to think that this time one year ago, I was just a normal girl. I was working a job I hated and wondering if that was all there was to my life: go to work, come home, go to sleep, wake up, go back to work, etc. On and on it went, with no end in sight.

Now I was a vampire, capable of astonishing things, living with the love of my eternal life. However, I was also near to being eradicated by a group of supernatural people with a compunction for showing up at the most inopportune times. The idea was absurd and laughable, enthralling and horrifying, as if we were living out a first-rate episode of Tales from the Crypt or the Outer Limits.

Yet, it was all terrifyingly true.

As we looked over the text, we focused on the first encounter with the SpellCasters...

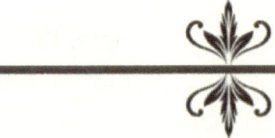

The year is 1440 A.D., and vampires continue to thrive all across the world. Throughout the countryside, we see colonies rising and new members being sired. This age of vampires is one of prosperity.

Yet a new threat exists. Enemies have risen against us. They call themselves the SpellCasters.

Magicians. Witches. Devils. These beings possess supernatural powers they use to hunt us. We have been powerless to stop them.

One of the London vampires came to us with stories of colony members disappearing, having been hunted down by these new foes. Some have literally vanished from the face of the earth. Others were violently attacked by the SpellCasters in broad daylight: setting them on fire, using wind to twist limbs apart, drowning them in their own blood, and burying what was left deep in the earth. These atrocities were witnessed by a handful of other colony members.

They have no fear. They provide no mercy. They appear to be without equal.

No one has seen anything like it before, and most unfortunately, it was not the last of them. Shortly afterwards, sightings of these vampire hunters arose in Germany, Romania, Morocco, Japan, and Egypt. More and more colonies have reported incidents.

Now we wait, here in Dublin, wondering when the SpellCasters will come for us. Will they kill all of us? Will any of us survive?

No one understands why the SpellCasters are attacking. There were no signs; they simply arrived one day and began their destruction of us, starting with the colony in Rennes, France. Why there? Is there a connection? Is that where they are from? We're uncertain.

All we know is that we survived the Inquisition, and we shall survive this.

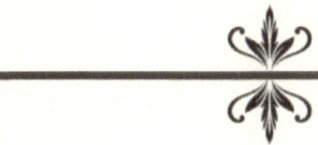

"Why Rennes?"

Michael glanced at me. "Perhaps that was where the first SpellCaster was created? Or maybe the first call to action was there?"

Kat was awe-struck by the information. "So long ago... Wow."

"Yes, and despite everything, it continues to be a mystery."

I turned my attention to Xander. "What do you think? You've been pretty quiet."

Xander was lost in thought, then glanced up to meet my eyes. He shook his head before he spoke. "Sorry, I was stuck on that last bit in the book."

"No worries."

"So we have the first report in 1440 A.D., nothing prior to that. What do we know about that time period?"

"About Europe?"

"Anything, really."

"Vampires?"

"Even better. What've you got?"

Michael interjected. "Based on the history I've studied, that's easy. Gilles de Rais was hanged in October of that year."

"Gilles de Rais?" Xander clearly hadn't heard of him; he looked perplexed.

"He was convicted of killing numerous children and summoning devils. But there are many who believe it was a conspiracy against him by the Church."

"How does this involve vampires?"

"There was a rumor that he ate the flesh of the children, thus adding 'vampire' to his legend."

"Yeah, that would do it."

Kat made a face. "Gross."

"But why would he be a trigger?" asked Xander.

A thought occurred to me. "Maybe... Maybe someone was retaliating for his death?"

Michael's eyes narrowed on mine, something he did when we were on the same page. "Consider that he was later deemed a victim of Church persecution. De Rais may have been a patsy for the vampire community, so—"

"Someone may have created the SpellCasters to enact revenge?" I finished.

"Yes, something like that."

Kat was on the edge of her seat. "Ooh. Now we're getting somewhere."

I was ruffled. "Great. One guy gets a bad deal and now the rest of us are paying for it. Nice. That's *totally* fair."

Xander looked confused. "That still doesn't explain why Ricky sent them after you two."

I leaned across the table and smacked him on the shoulder. "Didn't you hear? We're fabulous! Everyone wants a piece of this."

Everyone laughed except Michael. "No, Xander is right. Why would Ricky—a vampire—call them to come after us? He's one of our own. There has to be a more murderous explanation."

"The book says even vampires can hire them."

"You're missing my point: why would a vampire call on them to hunt another vampire? I think there's more to this."

My smile slowly faded. I loved my man, but his ability to be a buzzkill was tremendously annoying sometimes. "Thanks, Mike. Now I'm just as confused as I was before this conversation."

"Don't be. We're on the right path. I'm sure of it."

"You just think we're missing something."

"Yes."

I sighed. He was right. What would make Ricky want to have us killed, especially by a superior enemy like the SpellCasters? They were his enemy, too! That would be like a fish sending a shark after another fish: tremendously sketchy.

"Ooh..."

I perked up. "What is it Kat?"

"When you and Michael suggested someone had been retaliating for Gilles de Rais' death, I got an inkling."

Xander turned towards her and laughed. "You do have some powerful inklings! Spill it woman! We're all ears!"

I watched my beautiful friend Kat, her berry lips pulling tight as a sly smile crept across her face. I felt one of my eyebrows pop up.

"How old are you, Michael?"

Startled, Michael replied, "Over 250 years. I've kind of lost count."

"And your...uh... What do you call them? Your maker?"

Michael grimaced. "I'm not sure. She was probably a couple hundred herself, at least."

"Were you her only child? Er, progeny?"

"I don't know for certain. She spoke of other vampires, but I don't know if they were associates or her own. Why?"

I realized where Kat was going with this. "You don't think—"

"I do."

"Whoa..."

Xander was getting both excited and frustrated. "Alright damnit. Would you please tell us what the hell is going on?"

"Now—now wait a minute..." Michael started to put two and two together.

"I'm serious!" Kat was giddy and bounced in her seat.

"I think she's onto something, Mike."

Xander's eyes darted from one person to another so fast, I thought he would burst into flames. "I'm done. Would someone *please* tell me just what the fuck you're on about?"

Michael slapped a hand on Xanders back. "Here's the gist of it, friend. Kat's suggesting my sire was with Gilles de Rais and created the SpellCasters to punish other vampires."

"Okay... Wait. 'With'... As in lovers?"

"Yes."

"She blamed other vampires for his death? Twisted, but alright. What's that gotta do with Ricky?"

Kat piped up. "I think she sired someone who later found out that Michael killed her. They're pissed off and want revenge. That same progeny sired Ricky."

Xander's thoughts finally hit the mark. "And Ricky's been playing the long game to get to you." He turned his attention back to Michael. Michael bowed his head in agreement.

Slouching forward in my chair, I waved at Xander. "Hi! Don't mind me; I'm just along for the ride."

I quickly straightened up. "I say we get rid of these SpellCasters and then hunt Ricky down. We need to find out who his sire is. I'm tired of playing the victim here." Kat and I exchanged hi-fives, then I swiveled in my chair to face my love. "Whaddya say, Mike? Ready to be done with this mess?"

Michael grinned, his eyes dark and menacing. "Absolutely, love. Absolutely."

In Boston's warehouse district, a giant snake slithered out of the sewer, its forked tongue spitting forward to taste the air. Long and sleek, its sinewy form moved across dirt, gravel, and muck to enter a dilapidated building that once housed boat-making machinery. Inside the structure, it paused to collect itself into a circular pile, then moved along pallets and steel beams, hiding itself whenever possible in shadow.

At last, it slithered up to a pair of legs standing at the far end of the warehouse floor. Swathed in all black, the figure remained still as the snake circled its form. It stayed immobile as the reptile hissed and reared up in front of it. Without warning, a hand swiftly struck out and grabbed the snake behind its head. The serpent continued to hiss at the figure, but they refused to let go.

All at once, the snake began to change shape, transforming back into a human being. Before long, the serpent was gone and Ricky was left in its place, struggling to breath with the hand tight at his throat.

He choked and sputtered, grasping at the figure that held him inches from the ground.

"Please." Ricky's voice rasped as he squirmed. "I beg you."

The hand opened and released him. Ricky fell to the concrete and crumpled. Coughing, he looked up at the figure. "Thank you."

"Don't thank me just yet, boy."

"What are you going to do to me?"

The figure shook their head. "Once I learned of its existence, I waited decades for you to get the book from the Boston colony. I was terribly patient." The figure glared at Ricky, fixing their cold, dead eyes on him. "Now I learn you had it in your pitiful little hands and let them take it? What an atrocity."

"I'm sorry, I–"

"You *are* sorry. You're a sorry excuse for a vampire, Mr. Yun. I've travailed myself all these years, eager to enact my revenge. I've played the long game, waiting and waiting for the right moment. Now you let them swipe the *one source* of information that could lead them to victory over my sire's creation." The figure tsk-tsked at him. "You disappoint me..."

"I know, sire. I'm weak, and I didn't think–"

"No. You didn't *think*."

Ricky lowered his eyes and bowed his head. "What will you do with me?"

"I haven't decided that."

"Will you kill me?"

"Perhaps..."

After a few moments of devastating silence, the figure bent down and raised Ricky's head by his chin. He stared into their icy blue eyes, feeling the blood in his veins freeze over. He blinked rapidly, yet their gaze remained steady, unwavering and sinister.

"Live in fear."

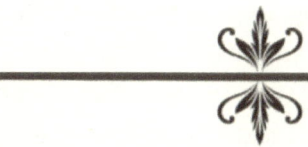

Night had fallen on Boston. Michael and I rode in silence, heading for home. We were ready to fight. No SpellCaster would get the drop on us this time. No sir, we were going to be prepared for them, come hell or high water.

We had left Kat and Xander in the hotel. They could sit this one out. Michael and I would be using our vampire abilities to defend ourselves and 'unleash hell' on the SpellCasters.

I went to turn the radio on in the car, and Michael smiled. "Yes, let's have some music." I returned the expression and found a great 80s track, "Take Me Home" by Phil Collins, on a local station. How apropos. My head tilted back against my headrest, and I sang softly while streetlights flashed across the dashboard.

"I love to hear you sing." I glanced at Michael, and he was still smiling. He turned to look at me—

All of a sudden, Michael's arm flew across my upper chest, pinning me to the seat. A car came barreling at us on our right, slamming into the passenger side of the vehicle and crunching into the framework. Our car was shoved backwards and began flipping over and over again. (Thank God for my seatbelt.) Skidding the last few feet, it finally came to rest upside down.

Just like that, my lights went out.

A few minutes later and groaning, I opened my eyes. My blurry vision gradually coalesced into a solid and I looked around. Michael was already climbing out, and he came around to my side and reached out for me. I reached up and unbuckled myself before grabbing his hand and letting him pull me out of the busted window. Cuts meant nothing; we were already healing.

"Are you alright?"

My head was pounding from a probable concussion. "I'm fine. What the hell— Who hit us? Are they okay?"

Immediately, Michael was surveying our surroundings. "There." He pointed to a silver SUV that had a huge dent crammed in its hood. It sat diagonally across the street from our position, smoke coming from its engine. The driver's side door was wide open. Blood decorated the dashboard.

The driver was gone.

No other cars were around. I appreciated the anonymity that came with the darkness of side streets. It meant we wouldn't have to explain the accident. All we had were ourselves, a foreclosed-on house, streetlights, and two busted vehicles.

All of a sudden, I heard a noise behind us. Spinning around, I saw a glint of metallic sheen under the sodium lighting and a slithering tail disappearing down a sewer grate up ahead. I ran over to the grate and bent down, shouting into the tunnels. "Coward! You're a fucking coward, Ricky!"

Michael came up behind me and put a hand on my shoulder. "Next time."

"I'm getting really sick and tired of his bullshit."

"I know, but we don't have time to get distracted by him."

"So now what?"

"Now, we go home."

Michael held out his right hand to me, and I took it without question. We walked over behind the house so no one could see us. There he took me in his arms, brushed some of my hair back from my face, and we traveled home.

As soon as we arrived, I kissed him, feeling a need to touch him and feel his lips against mine. The accident had spooked me a little, and it was vital that I take a minute to appreciate him. His hands came up, and while one held my upper right arm and pulled me close, the other handheld the back of my head so that he could deepen our kiss.

He was so warm, and his mouth was setting me on fire. I found myself breathless in moments, and when I broke the kiss, he was breathless, too.

A moment later, we were walking toward the house. Inside, we began fortifying everything: doors, windows, even the bloody fireplaces. Guns were pulled from the armory cabinets in the library. Least of all, we made sure our abilities were firing on all cylinders.

Getting everything ready was easy. We had all of our ducks in a row. Waiting for the SpellCasters to arrive was the hard part, and waiting games were my least favorite games to play.

Michael grabbed the blood pouches, and I grabbed the wine glasses. We pulled two chairs up to one of our picture windows in the kitchen, and Michael poured our drinks. Handing me my glass, he bent down and pressed a kiss to the top of my head. I sighed and leaned back in my chair, propping my feet up on the window ledge. Michael sat down next to me and took a sip from his own glass, leaning back in his chair with his legs spread wide. The sky continued to brighten one foot candle at a time.

"It's been a while since we've watched the sun come up." I sipped from my glass, appreciating the joys of fresh A-positive blood.

"That it has."

"I hope this won't be our last."

"Never."

"We can't know for sure. Tomorrow could be the end of us, you know."

"It would take more than some devil sorcery to stop us, now wouldn't it?"

"Devil sorcery?" I gave a light smack to his arm. "You're such a handsome antique."

He chuckled. "I'm serious. You and I can be quite formidable together. Now that we know they're coming, we're prepared, and they won't have the chance to wound us like before. We're actually a threat to them."

"Are you calling us a vampiric force to be reckoned with? A dynamic duo?"

"I think they are going to have a hard time getting rid of us."

"You make it sound like we're invincible, and if that's true, I am so down for that life... Ooh, we could do *extra* naughty things if that's the case. Mmm..." I winked at him and waggled my eyebrows. He laughed, and I turned my attention back to the rich hues permeating the skyline. Everything was suddenly so beautiful...

I felt, rather than saw, Michael reach out and take my left hand. A moment later, I felt something slip on my ring finger. Startled, I looked down and there was the most spectacular piece of jewelry I had ever seen: a platinum band studded in evenly spaced diamonds with three pinkish-red garnets between some of them. I looked up at Michael's face, and he was just watching me, his face reserved but his eyes glowing with anticipation.

The ring looked nearly identical to the wedding ring my grandmother had.

"Is this...? I mean, are you asking...?"

"I am."

"Then I do!"

"You do?"

"One hundred thousand percent! Yes!"

Michael grinned and leaned across to kiss me, his hand never leaving mine. Using my kiss to reassure him, I felt every bit of tension leave him and he relaxed. Every ounce of his excitement was in that kiss, and when he pulled back, he was still grinning from ear to ear. I'd never seen him look so happy.

"Mr. Hawkins," I said nodding to him.

"Mrs. Hawkins." He nodded back.

I lifted his hand to my lips and kissed the back of it. "I love you."

"And I you. Always."

"Always," I whispered back with a smile.

We watched the sunrise and continued our vigil, holding each other's hand, knowing the future was out of our control. Soon enough, we would find out what our fate was.

Chapter Seventeen

Finality

There was a knock at the door, and I felt my stomach flip.

It was time.

Michael and I stood up from our kitchen chairs. The morning light was in full effect outside, and the sky was a beautiful blue. We looked at each other, pushed our chairs underneath the table, and took our glasses to the sink. I rinsed them and put them in the dishwasher.

Are you ready?

As ready as I'll ever be. I laughed. *Do you think we can get a trophy if we win?*

Who knows? We may be the first vampires in history to defeat them.

Wow. That's an impressive thought. Should we share what works with others?

I think we should share it with the Boston colony. Besides, we do need to return their book to them.

Michael smiled and held out his left hand. I took it happily, his palm rough and warm against my own. Together, we headed towards the main hall.

The knocking on the door increased in frequency and intensity until it had become a relentless banging, loud and boisterous. Cautiously we approached the front door. My stomach had twisted into knots, but I knew what I had to do.

Stretching intentionally yet leisurely, I transformed my body, hands becoming gigantic, fat paws and skin becoming soft, dark fur. My jaw stretched and widened, with extra teeth joining the ones already inside my mouth. My tongue grew broad and coarse, and I licked the lengthy whiskers that had formed on either side of my smile. Having fully morphed into a panther, my eyesight was far greater than it had been in my human form. Everything was in sharply contrasting black and white, including Michael. He was watching me in fascination and smiling, never ceasing to be amazed by my unique ability. Then he turned his attention to the door, his face becoming menacing and shadowed.

Suddenly the door blew open, a burst of wind barreling through the hallway and hurling dry leaves toward us. I turned my head to the side to avoid the brunt of it in my face. Turning back, I saw the three SpellCasters stepping through the doorway, one after the other.

It was like a hazy nightmare.

My memory of their first 'visit' to our home thrust itself to the forefront of my mind, and I saw them as they had been: stunning and exotic, intoxicating but frightening. With intensity, I recalled how the four of them had entrapped us, slithering vines everywhere and elemental powers laying waste to who we were. I couldn't bear to have that happen again. Instinctively, my body took a step backwards when I should have moved forwards.

At that moment, I felt Michael's hand on my back, stroking my fur, and it felt soothing, calming. I purred and then swung my attention back to the enemy. I had already vowed that this would be the end, and I would see it through.

I relinquished myself to the beast I had become and stamped my right front paw on the floor. Scraping my claws along the wood, I let out a furious roar, daring them to come after me. The smallest one with long, silvery blonde hair was startled, flinching and going stock still where she stood. The tall man held out a hand and touched her, shaking his head. She looked at him and nodded before turning her attention back to us.

The tall woman had a sneer on her face, and she was stalking Michael, coming down the landing steps. I lept in front of him and snarled at her, waiting for her to work her magic. She froze, unsure of what to do with me. All of a sudden, she snarled back, and I felt my ears perk up. How curious... I didn't think she was capable of transformation, so I began to step forward.

Before my paw hit the ground in front of me, the tall woman began to cast and weave, her hands twisting and intertwining. She was chanting low and fast, her words unknown to me. I growled a warning to her, but she didn't stop. Her words kept coming and a glow began to emanate from her fingertips. The next thing I knew, fireballs were hurtling toward us from her palms.

Flinging myself to the side, I felt one of the fireballs singe my fur, eliciting a howl from me; I was enraged. Charging toward her, she swiped her hands up through the air. A wall of fire rose up between us, glowing bright and exuding an enormous amount of heat. It stopped a foot away from the ceiling. Skidding to a halt in front of it, the flames seared the very tip of my nose. I backpedaled and growled as she stood there, smiling and blowing kisses at me from the other side. The bitch was too cocky for her own good.

I glanced to my right and saw Michael fending off blades made of ice. The small one had been throwing little handmade daggers at him, weaving her hands and then hurling her creations in his direction. Michael smacked some away before drawing out the gun at his back. He fired at her, but she deflected the impact by raising a column of ice from the landing floor. The bullet shattered the column on impact, and as he continued to fire his gun, new columns burst upward. Again and again, she shielded herself from the bullets until Michael's clip was empty.

The tall man swirled his left hand in the air and swiped his other hand along his arm. Suddenly we were unable to breathe. I felt the air leave my lungs in a rush, and all at once, we were struggling, desperately trying to inhale oxygen. I couldn't roar, couldn't speak, falling down where I stood, and watching as Michael did the same.

Close to passing out, I saw Michael slam his hand down on the floor. To my right, the ground trembled and cracked open. Smoke rose from within, and a tremendously sized demon crawled out from the underworld. It was a behemoth, four feet long at its widest point and eight feet tall, muscular and burnt orange in color. The demon bore four gray-colored horns on its head and four glowing yellow eyes—two of each on either side of its face. Its teeth were like miniature daggers in its mouth, split into double rows, with four curved, extra-long ones descending from the upper jaw. In place of its hands were giant claws, similar to those of a sloth but extra sharp and dangerous. The demon's chest was criss-crossed with scars and steel chains, covering it like over-sized chainmail armor. At the base of its squat legs were wide, flat feet with eight toes.

As soon as the demon finished climbing out of the crack in the floor, it let out a thunderous roar unlike anything I have ever heard. The tall man was taken aback by its appearance, and his hands froze mid-air. The tall woman doubled back to her previous position, curling her lip at the new arrival. In fact, all three SpellCasters stopped what they were doing and retreated into defensive postures.

I felt oxygen rush back into my lungs as the tall man's spell ceased working. Panting, I rolled onto my stomach and pushed myself up. Michael followed suit, rising to stand tall, and ready to square off against our foes. I smiled at them, knowing what was coming next.

Before I could enact my plan, I began to feel anger, and it was unlike any fury I had experienced before: strong, violent, eager. This was new, red-hot, and it was burning a hole inside of me, this raging, seething hatred. Any contempt I had felt for the SpellCasters was waning. I growled low in my throat, feeling my frame vibrate, as I turned towards...Michael.

He was staring at me, his eyes hooded, and his lips pulled back in a snarl. He hunched down, low and balanced, preparing to attack. I leaned back and then pounced, throwing my huge body at him, claws out and ready to strike. He held an arm out to deflect the blow, but it did little against my beast form. Raking my claws across his chest, I sliced into his flesh and heard him yell. Successfully hurting my prey, I was euphoric and continued to attack, biting his arm and shaking him while my teeth dug into his muscles. He slashed and kicked at me, but I ignored it. I was determined to drench him in his own blood. It wasn't long before he fell to the floor, defeated. My jaws gaping wide, I prepared to bite down on his head, ready for the crunch and telltale popping sensation.

"Celie, no!"

I heard a voice call out to me, and keeping a paw on my prey, I shifted my sight to my left. A transparent figure was standing in the hall just a dozen feet away. Immediately, I recognized her.

It was Fiadh.

"Ya canna do this, *cailin*!"

I struck out at my prey and knocked him unconscious. Chuffing, I trotted over to my friend and sat in front of her. She eyed me with such shock and sadness, I tilted my head as if to ask her why.

"Aye, love. I am sad. Ye're spelled. They have ye fightin' yer true love. Break free, *cailin*."

I turned around and looked at my prey, which was beginning to push itself back up off the floor. I looked beyond it and saw the small one chanting and shifting her hands to and fro. I snapped my head back to look at Fiadh.

"Yes. *She* is yer real enemy! Ignore yer anger for Michael. Destroy the nasty Caster!"

I stood up, shook out my fur, and slowly turned around, feeling as if I was fighting against a current. My body desired to finish off my prey, to slice him open and spill out his insides on the hallway floor. I sniffed the air and was invigorated by the scent of his blood. However, I trusted Fiadh, and if she said he was not my enemy, I knew in my gut that I had to fight what I was feeling.

Instead, I focused on the small one near the door. She was rotating her hands and warping her fingers into various shapes as she whispered her magical words. As I approached, she watched me and stopped. I growled, warning her of what was coming. She squeaked and began manipulating her hands again, water droplets coalescing in the air into a spiral shape. A spike of water formed from within the center and shot at me. Then another. I easily dodged them. Preparing to pounce, I glared at her and bared my teeth.

Without warning, I was pummeled on my left side by...nothing? There was literally nothing there. I swung my gaze forward to see the tall man was controlling the air again. He proceeded to hurl bursts of it into my side. I wailed and fell to the floor.

By distracting the small one, I had managed to break the control she had over Michael, too. Already healed from my bite wounds, he rushed over to me and took the brunt of several air shots, bracing himself as he was pummeled. I glanced up at him, desperate for him to forgive me, and I could see in his eyes that he felt the same—concerned about what had transpired between us.

Through all of this, the tall woman had remained standing behind her wall of fire. The demon had proceeded to her position and began striking out at her through the flames, undamaged by the heat. The tall woman shrieked and ducked, using her smaller frame to dodge the blows and avoid getting hit by the demon. While at the demon's back, she aimed her hands at the ceiling and sent a steady blaze upward and around the chandelier hanging above us. Within moments, the heavy and dangerous glass decoration was freed and came crashing down atop the demon's head, knocking it out.

With Michael blocking me from the tall man's assault, I rose to my feet and stared him down. He and the small one were now in my sights and would pay for what they had done. I closed my eyes, hearing Michael grunt next to me with each hit, and shifted my mental focus to call on them: the ghosts, the wraiths, the banshees, and the poltergeists. Even still, I didn't call just one; no, I called *all of them*.

I heard voices, hushed and quiet, whispering just behind my ear. A breeze fluttered by my right flank. Out of nowhere, a scream pierced the veil between our world and theirs, and I opened my eyes. They were *everywhere*. All around us were transparent figures: some standing, some floating, some flying above our heads just beneath the ceiling. Where some were white, others were green, and some were blue. A wailing banshee passed close by, skimming my head, and I was awestruck by it. A poltergeist silently hurtled a vase past Michael and towards the tall woman. The sound of it hitting the wall broke the awesome hold the impressive display had held over everyone. A literal wall of ghosts came storming towards the SpellCasters, ready to overwhelm them and drown them in ectoplasm.

I glanced at Michael, both of us amazed at the powerful display. Hoping the spirits would aid in our defense, we both planned our next strike. However, one of the SpellCasters had different plans.

The tall woman crouched down where she was just beneath the landing stairway and began casting, her hands moving faster and faster as she slowly rose higher and higher. Shooting up into a standing position, she flung out her arms, her fingers splayed wide on her hands. A firestorm shot forth from them and sprayed the specters as if she was using a flame-thrower. I watched as liquid fire flowed out of her fingertips, striking the ghosts and causing them to evaporate.

Adding to the chaos, she began spontaneously combusting any transparent specter she could land her eyes on. Her eyes glowed white-hot like energized flames, ready to consume every living thing in her path. As she focused them on a single ghost, it would simply *poof* out of existence, leaving a mere whisp in its place. Numerous souls disappeared as soon as they had arrived, with nary a cry or shout.

The tall woman's face bore a depraved and terrible grin, wide and diabolical, showcasing her devious joy at destruction and mayhem. She went back and forth, dispatching phantoms with her magical fire as easily as striking a match. Tilting her head back, a war-cry erupted from her tart cherry lips.

However, in all her calamitous glee, the tall woman paid no mind to the side-effects of her spells. From the corner of my eye, I saw the tall man and the small one beginning to claw at their throats. Their eyes were panic-stricken, desperation written across their faces. Before long, they each collapsed, their mouths agape and chests heaving.

They were suffocating.

Watching her pyromania, I remembered a time when a fireman had come to my grade school. He had explained how oxygen fuels fires, with fire eating up all the available oxygen in the process. Any oxygen in the vicinity of the SpellCaster was being sucked into the fire and replaced with poisonous fumes. These fumes and lack of oxygen were permeating the area just behind her, where her brethren stood.

In her zest for devastation, the tall woman was killing her own kind.

I shifted back into human form, uncaring that I was standing in the hallway in all my naked glory. Was it cold? Yes. Did I care? Not in the least.

"Hey, you are *brilliant*, you know that?"

She stopped her pyrotechnics and glared at me. "How dare you speak to me, you git!"

"How dare I *speak* to you?" I shook my head in disbelief. "Maybe you should pay better attention to what you're doing?"

"I'm destroying your pitiful little ghosties, that's what I'm doing." She laughed and resumed taking out every soul that stepped forward. When each one was destroyed, another two took its place, but she paid little mind to that. She believed her powers were unstoppable.

"Ahem…" I cleared my throat and pointed to where her SpellCaster friends were lying on the floor, just behind her on the landing.

Immediately, she ceased 'firing' and rushed over to the bodies on the floor, crouching down to learn they were no longer of this world. "No. No no no!" She began crying tears of sadness at having lost her friends. They were dead, recklessly killed by her own actions.

Yet those same tears turned into ones of anger as she sought to blame someone for their death. Pivoting to her right, she focused her attention on me. "*You…*" she seethed, gritting her teeth and hissing the word at me. "You've done this!" Spittle came flying out of her mouth along with her accusation.

"Me? I was standing over here." I pointed to the very spot on which I was standing.

"You tricked me!"

"And just how did she do that?" Michael came forward to stand behind me, placing his hands on my upper arms. In the cold of the hallway, his hands were toasty and comfortable against my bare skin.

"You know damn well how this cheeky bitch did it! She unleashed her spirits on us!"

"Seems to me it was *your* attack that caused the real damage here."

Standing upright, the tall woman glared at us, her eyes blazing with fiendish hatred. Slowly, and with hostile intent, she proceeded to stalk toward us. The oversized demon moved near her feet, finally coming to, but she merely glanced at it, and it burst into flames from within. Apparently, its skin was the real barrier to hellfire; as we watched, its internal organs liquified and leaked out of its orifices. It collapsed with a heavy thud on the cracked hallway floor. Its skin caved in on itself under the weight of the 'chainmail', leaving nothing but an empty, leathery husk.

Michael and I stood our ground, letting the devil fire-bitch weave her way around the demon carnage to come towards us.

Are we really doing this?

Yes. It's the only way.

I'm scared, Mike.

Me, too. But the sooner we do this, the sooner it will all be over.

With those thoughts echoing in my mind, I braced myself for what I knew was coming: an attempt at revenge.

The lone SpellCaster stopped ten feet away from us and raised her hands. Twisting her hands over each other in rapid succession, she brought them to her lips and blew into them. As she did, smoke began to rise from within her hands.

I had seen this before. She was going to split us apart again. I felt panic rearing its ugly head. Michael squeezed my upper arms, alerting me that he was ready to strike. I steeled myself to remain where I was, unmoving. I pushed down the panic and the fear.

As soon as the SpellCaster pushed her arms forward, we rushed her, taking her by surprise. I took her right arm and Michael took her left. We dragged her backwards, kicking and screaming out the front door towards the fountain.

Her spell wasn't completely gone, and she let her arms ignite. Michael and I were ablaze within moments, and I screamed at the pain. Feeling the burning, searing heat encompass me, my skin sizzled and my hair was gone in seconds. Michael also cried out, his beautiful skin blistering from the fire.

Even still, we persisted in our pursuit of the fountain. Reaching the stone border of it, we heaved and shoved the last SpellCaster into the pale blue waters. She wailed, her arms instantly put out, and our own fires were doused. Our grips tight, I glanced at Michael, and he nodded. Together we pushed her to the bottom of the fountain waters and held her down. She thrashed and flailed, jerking and trying to pull away from us, water splashing about and drenching any last part of us that had been inflamed.

I watched her, watched as the bubbles grew fewer around her face, and then as they stopped rising to the surface. On her face was an expression of surprise, as if she never expected to die this way. After a minute or two, I cautiously released her arm, part of me afraid that she would spring back to life like villains do in the movies. Fortunately for me, she did no such thing.

Looking up at Michael, I thought I saw what I was feeling written on his own face. He turned his gaze up to me, and we simply regarded each other. We were both an unholy mess, but both of us only cared about what was in our eyes.

I fell back a little, thunking my naked ass on the cold edge of the fountain. "Now what?"

"Now what, indeed." Michael sat down on the ledge, too. We were quite a pair, what with our vicious burns, missing hair, and a drowned SpellCaster between us.

"Is it possible it's all really over?"

"Not quite."

"What the hell is left?"

"Ricky, and whoever sired him."

"Damn that Ricky..." I splashed a little water with my hand, frustrated that we couldn't put all of this behind us already.

"We'll find him, and then we'll show his sire why they should've left well enough alone..." Michael's words did little to hide his lingering anger. The SpellCasters may have been taken care of, but it was our unknown enemy that infuriated him, and it was someone who needed to fear what we would bring to the table.

"Well, shall we?" I gestured to the house. Michael stood up and held his arm out for me. I took it happily, and we walked back inside our home.

Chapter Eighteen

Most Tiresome

"Come back here, you bastard!"

I shouted after Ricky, who was running fast through the house's landscape maze. He was a quick little bugger. I had to stop to catch my breath more than once.

He had tried to attack us at home, sneaking through a ventilation shaft into the side of the house. We don't have alarms, so it was quite a surprise. Imagine finding a giant snake slithering through your main hallway on its way to the library. We knew he wanted the SpellCaster text, but hadn't expected him to break in. The act was just desperate and stupid.

Despite the state of disarray our home was in, he was unaware we had already killed the SpellCasters a few days earlier.

Now Ricky ran through our maze in human form (naked, of course), high tailing it amongst the bushes to try to escape us. Michael was already in pursuit, and I was getting ready to shift into my panther form to keep up with him. I needed speed and it was obvious I couldn't keep up on human legs.

Do you see him?

No. Do you?

I hope we didn't lose him.

He couldn't have gotten far.

Still...I wish I could fly overhead like Marcus.

Who the hell is Marcus?

A vampire friend of mine.

Okay, we really need to have a talk about the people you know and what you don't tell me.

I promise. Right now, we need to find Ricky.

No worries, Mike. I'm on it.

Knowing that panthers had a stronger sense of smell, I shed my clothes and morphed into my beloved beast mode. I relished the sensation of shifting from a buxom human into a sleek, humongous black cat: fur replacing skin, claws replacing nails. If only I could walk about in this form every day...

Well, I could, but I couldn't go out into town, that's for sure. A panther walking through Bantum would surely send the residents into fits of hysteria. I wasn't prepared to be responsible for that just yet.

Once I was fully transformed, I sniffed the air, seeking Ricky's scent on the wind. As soon as I captured it, I plodded off in his direction, taking my time and pausing every now and then to redirect based on his movement. I wasn't beholden to the maze layout: I traversed through the bushes and over them without a care. It didn't take long to locate him, huddled in a corner between two tall hedges. I snarled at him and bayed for Michael.

After a moment, Michael came sauntering around the corner, looking ruggedly handsome as ever in his khaki pants, brown t-shirt and matching boots. I chuffed for him as he approached. Nothing could diminish my feelings for him, not even my existence as a panther. He extended a hand as he passed, stroking my fur and eliciting a low rumbling purr from me.

"Well, well, Ricky... You came for the book, I take it?"

Ricky said nothing. He simply stood there, watching us—me in particular. I focused my emerald green eyes on him and stretched, preparing to pounce if needed.

"We still have it, but it will do you no good. The SpellCasters have been destroyed."

At those words, Ricky flinched. He looked over at Michael, trying to stare him down unsuccessfully.

"I need to return the book. I don't want the Boston colony after me. They've already come looking for it."

"Oh, is that all?" Michael paused as Ricky nodded. "We thought it was because of *your sire.*"

In an instant, Ricky looked rocked to his core. "What... What are you talking about?"

"We know, Ricky." Michael gestured to me and himself. "We know all about their plan to enact revenge against me. Just tell me who it is, and this can all be over."

Ricky tried to laugh, but it vibrated in his throat, and he ended up sounding shaky and unsteady. "You're crazy. My sire is dead. Dead and gone these last 50 years."

"I highly doubt that."

"It's true! They were killed by a vampire hunter in San Francisco!"

I growled at Ricky, tired of his games and his lies. Michael put a hand on my head to urge me to be calm. I understood but didn't care for the slow pace. I stomped in place, impatient for us to get on with things.

"Celie is growing anxious. She's exhausted from having to hunt you down, Ricky. I can't promise that she won't take your demise into her own...paws."

Ricky eyed me warily. "I swear to you, my sire is no more."

I howled, loud and powerful, ready to strike. Michael took the steps needed to close the distance between himself and Ricky. Grabbing

Ricky by the neck, he held him up in the air, Ricky's feet dangling off the ground. Eyes wide as saucers, Ricky grasped Michael's hand, struggling to hold on.

"Enough! Who is your sire!"

"They're dead!"

Michael squeezed Ricky's throat. "Tell me!"

"I...can't..."

"Tell me now, or so help me, I'll wring it from you..."

Ricky merely choked and sputtered. "Please... I can't...breathe... Please..."

I watched as Michael had enough and dropped Ricky, letting him fall to the ground. Michael turned around, his face an expression of disgust, while Ricky coughed and inhaled deep, eager breaths. As Michael walked away, I took that moment to walk over to where Ricky lay on the ground.

Putting my snout directly in his face, I gave a sharp exhale and placed a paw on his chest, letting the full weight of my body ease down onto him. Ricky froze, his movements coming to a standstill. My claws came out, and instinctively, I flexed my paw. I stared into his eyes and growled, low and menacing, letting him know that I had the power to kill him. Then I released him and returned to Michael's side a few feet away.

"Leave." Michael pointed to the exit of the maze not 20 feet from us. "Leave now and never come back."

Ricky scrambled to his feet and practically sprinted towards the exit.

"If we see you anywhere near us again, Celie will make good on her promise."

I roared in agreement. Ricky looked over his shoulder at us, then continued to frantically, haphazardly run for the exit. Once he was out of sight, I shifted back into my human form, missing the feel of fur across my body.

"I hope this is really, truly the last that we see of him. I'm not sure I could handle another round of this with him."

"Only time will tell."

"I wish we had learned the name of his sire. It's incredibly frustrating to be so close to the answer and have it run away, practically screaming."

"I know, but I couldn't have killed him."

I smiled at Michael, knowing that no matter what, he had a level of morality that was unbreakable. "I know that, silly. I'm not blaming you. It just demonstrated how powerful a bond there can be between a sire and their progeny."

"We have such a bond."

"True, but ours is so much more than that." I took his hand, and we walked to where I had left my clothes. As I put them on, something in Michael's eyes twinkled.

"Oh no, mister, we still have to finish cleaning up the house."

Michael grinned. "I can't help myself. You know that."

I returned his smile and leaned up to kiss him. "I can't say I blame you. I am super dishy."

Michael laughed. As I turned to head to the house, he playfully smacked my ass, and I giggled.

"Last one there has to get naked!" I yelled, then ran to the house with Michael fast at my heels.

The house was in shambles. Lying on the outskirts of Bantum, it had been built over one hundred years ago by the family of a publishing house empire. Yet, the last few years had left it in disarray. It was falling apart.

Ricky stepped over the threshold and went inside, nervous about having to explain what happened at the Hawkins estate. He looked around but was unable to see much. The corners of the house, dark and foreboding, were filled with cobwebs and dust. The floorboards creaked underneath his feet with every step. He flinched as a bird took flight from deeper within the room, flying into one of the side rooms. Everything about the place told Ricky it was bad, that he should leave right away, but he stayed.

Stopping in the middle of the great room, Ricky called out to his sire. "I'm here! I've come!"

There was a shuffling noise, and his sire came from out of the same side room, moving slowly and deliberately. They circled him, tsk-tsking at his disheveled state. Ricky hung his head down low, embarrassed.

"Do you have the book?"

"No, sire."

"Why not?"

Further embarrassed at having to admit his capture, Ricky's face flushed bright red. "They found me. I couldn't get to it."

"This is getting to be most tiresome."

"There's more."

After a minute or two of silence on Ricky's part, his sire spoke up. "Well? Get on with it!"

Ricky cleared his throat. "The, uh, the SpellCasters are...um...dead."

"What!"

"The SpellCasters are dead."

"I heard you the first fucking time, Mr. Yun."

"Yes, sire."

"How?"

"I'm not sure. I just know that Hawkins and the girl have admitted to destroying them."

Ricky's sire held a hand up, signaling for him to stop talking. Ricky again bowed his head, staring at his sneakers in abject silence. He knew this was a horrible thing, the destruction of the SpellCasters, and he wanted to help his sire using any possible means. However, he knew he couldn't face Michael and Celie again. He had no desire to die.

Yet death was the only thing on his sire's mind: death of the other vampires, the death of their own sire's creation, and now a new death was pushing its way up to the surface, clawing for release.

As Ricky stood still, pondering how he could help his sire, they morphed the fingers of their left hand into wickedly sharp talons. Reaching out swiftly, smoothly, they swung their left arm out and sliced across Ricky's throat. Shocked, Ricky's hand flew to his neck and tried to stop the blood flow; it was of no use. His lifeblood flowed fast and freely down his chest and pants onto the dank and dirty floor.

His sire stepped back, away from the death now leaking across the floorboards. A squeaking sound soon followed, and a swarm of rats flooded the room, sinking their teeth into Ricky's flesh. Ricky collapsed into a heap of ruin, what was left of his breath exhaling in one final act before ceasing altogether. His eyes glazed over: translucent, lifeless. Ricky Yun would cause no one any trouble anymore.

There, in the ramshackle house, what was once Ricky's sire walked around him and headed towards the front door. As they reached the doorframe, they turned around, examining the remnants of a lonely previous life. They sighed and proceeded to exit the building, heading towards a dark, bulky, and expensive SUV.

A large, masculine vampire stepped out of the passenger side door, reaching back to open the rear door for them. He had the distinct presence of mind to bow to them. The sire climbed in, and the vampire closed their door. Climbing back into the passenger seat, the vampire shut their own door, and the vehicle drove off into the night.

"Is everything set?"

"Yes, sire."

"Good."

"Where are we headed to?"

"All in good time. For now, just drive."

"Yes, sire."

Ricky's sire missed their own sire, Amelia Langston. Amelia had been ruthless, cunning, devious; a monstrous vampire that wreaked havoc amongst the ages. Had she only lived, perhaps things would have been different. Perhaps the SpellCasters would have led to an uprising among vampires—to taking over the cities rather than living in the shadows.

If only...

In the darkness of the backseat, Ricky's sire pulled out a cell phone and began checking their bank statements and stocks. Everything was coming together, and the money was pouring in from the latest scientific discovery. Lingering laboratory samples from a failed cult had proven most useful, and now vampire blood would be the boon of the century, leading to even more discoveries society could benefit from.

Soon it would be time to divest of the accounts and investments, to 'close up shop' if you will, and get down to the true plan: revenge for the death of Amelia. Now that the SpellCasters were dead, Ricky's sire would simply have to take care of things themselves. Once everything was closed out, there would be more time to devote to the cause.

After passing the Bantum business district, they reached up and tapped the shoulder of the front seat twice.

"Yes, sire?"

"Change direction. We're heading to see the Boston colony."

"The Boston colony?"

"Did I stutter?"

"No, sire." The driver made a U-turn at the nearest intersection and then headed for the interstate.

Once they were on the highway, the sodium lighting reached into the SUV, casting an orange glow every 50 feet. Ricky's sire glanced up into the rearview mirror, staring at their own eyes, watching the glow cross their face. Inside them was a burning need to finish this. One day, Michael Hawkins would be dead, and this would all be over.

Their cell phone rang. Looking away from the mirror, the sire—a woman—answered it. "Cressida Hawkins."

SHANNA ROBILLARD

FINIS

Foreign Language Guide

D◈: (pronounced 'doh-ah') In Twi (a dialect of the Akan language) of southern Ghana
and the Ivory Coast, this means 'love'.

Roscommon: (pronounced 'ruh-skah-munn') In Ireland, this is a county in Connacht, part of Northern Ireland, and it is very centrally located within the country.

Diamhair: (pronounced 'dee-uh-wer') In Irish, this means 'mystery'.

Éire: (pronounced 'ay-ruh') In Irish, this means Ireland.

Sliabh: (pronounced 'shlee-uv') In Irish, this means mountain.

Mo bhaile: (pronounced 'muh bah-leh') In Irish, this means 'my home'.

Seaicéad: (pronounced 'shack-aid') In Irish, this means 'jacket'.

Fiadh: (pronounced 'fee-ah') In Irish, this is a very popular girl's name that means 'deer' or 'wild'.

Dia Dhuit: (pronounced 'jee-ah-gwitch' or 'jee-ah-gwit') In Irish, this means 'hello'.

Tús: (pronounced 'toose') In Irish, this means 'beginnings.'

Teach Pairceanna Glasa: (pronounced 'chokh par-kenna glass-uh') In Irish, this means 'green fields house' or 'green park house'.

Go Mhaith: (pronounced 'guh mah') In Irish, this means 'good' or 'well' as a response when someone asks how you are.

SHANNA ROBILLARD

Tá Fáilte Romhat: (pronounced 'taw foyle-cheh roh-ot')
In Irish, this is equivalent to saying 'you're welcome' when
someone thanks you for something.

Oíche mhaith: (pronounced 'ee-hih mah') In Irish, this means
'goodnight'.

Daanav: (pronounced 'duh-uh-nuv') In India, this means 'demon'
or 'monster'.

Ionsáiteán: (pronounced 'in-suh-tun') In Irish, this means 'insert'.

Cailín amaideach: (pronounced 'coll-een ah-muh-duke ') In Irish,
this means 'silly girl'.

Madra Agus Caróg: (pronounced 'mah-druh ah-gus car-ohg ') In
Irish, this means 'dog and crow'

Mo shíorghra: (pronounced 'muh heer-graw') In Irish, this means
'my eternal love' or 'soulmates'.

Maidin mhaith: (pronounced 'my-din mah') In Irish, this means
'good morning'.

Paryaapt: (pronounce 'pee-ar-ee-ah-pee-tee') In Hindi, this means
'enough'.

Pavitr maan mujh par najar: (pronounced 'pah-vit-er
mahn mooj par nah-jar') In Hindi, this means 'sacred
mother watch over me'.

Grønn Utsikt: (pronounced 'gron oot-sick') In Norwegian, this
means 'green view'.

Tusen takk: (pronounced 'too-sen tak') In Norwegian, this means
'thank you so much'.

Vær så god: (pronounced 'var-sha-good) In Norwegian, this
means 'be so good' but is often used to mean 'you are
welcome'.

Sommerfugl: (pronounced 'sah-mare-foo-gul') In Norwegian, this means 'butterfly'.

Sykehus: (pronounced 'sick-uh-hoos') In Norwegian, this means 'hospital'.

Ta en drink på meg: (pronounced 'tah en drink poh meg') In Norwegian, this means 'have a drink on me'.

Viraam: (pronounced 'vur-ah-amm') In Hindi, this means 'stop'.

Pishaach: (pronounced 'pish-ah-ach') In Hindi, this means 'vampire' or 'flesh-eating monster'.

About the Author

Shanna C. Robillard is an award-winning author of fiction books, mostly in the romance genre. Having grown up with books by Dean Koontz, Stephen King, Piers Anthony, and Johanna Lindsey, she's read all kinds: horror, romance, fantasy, and the occasional educational one, too.

Her heart will always belong to sexy vampires, though.

A Virginia native, she currently resides in central New York state with her husband and a four-legged beastie.

You can see all of her books and how to contact her by visiting www.shannacrobillard.com.

www.ingramcontent.com/pod-product-compliance
Lightning Source LLC
Chambersburg PA
CBHW032040240626
47154CB00003B/1005